Willesd

New Short Stories 3

www.pretendgenius.com

Published simultaneously in the United States and Great Britain in 2011
by Pretend Genius Press
London, New York, San Francisco, Seattle, Washington D.C.

Edited by Stephen Moran

ISBN 978-0-9747261-5-1

Willesden Herald

New Short Stories 5

Pretend Genius Press

London, New York, San Francisco, Seattle, Washington D.C.

Acknowledgements

Many thanks to Maggie Gee and to Willesden Green Writers' Group for generously supporting the international Willesden Herald short story competition, 2011.

Stephen Moran

Hazel,

Best wishes - enjoy!

Angela

Y. J. Zhu

Apartment

Ever since her son moved out, Li An had lived alone in a large room facing west in the east wing of a *si he yuan*, a traditional courtyard housing in Beijing. She had lived in the same room, without running water, without kitchen, without bathroom for forty-five years. In the afternoons, the setting sun used to peel the colors off her room, now she rarely felt the heat of it. Late autumn had just passed. She was bracing for the cold winter.

The courtyard, hidden deep in a maze of winding old *hu tongs* near the Rear Lake behind the Forbidden City, had once belonged to a minor mandarin of the court. It was one of the rare courtyards with front, back, and middle enclosures. Li An's room was in the front enclosure. The middle and back ones were recently flattened to make way for an office building.

Li An stood in front of her window looking at a door opening to the pathways that ran along the north wing, waiting for it to open; the noises of the metropolis safely shielded away by the enclosing gray brick walls. A row of glass jars lined her windowsill, surgical tape labeled each in traditional calligraphy with old neighbors' names, all filled with loose change. There was space left for one more jar. Li An remembered the mornings when the courtyard was full of children playing hide-and-seek, the evenings when elders sat fanning themselves, gossiping, telling ghost stories to unnerve the young. This was almost the time of the year to bring in the goldfish.

The rising sun, looking meager and vague behind a veil of fog, resembled a pancake. A lone persimmon tree stood in the center of the courtyard, a pile of junk reposing at its base. Ripening fruits dotted the nearly bare branches, giving the courtyard the color of life. A whisper of wind blew from the northeast, a persimmon fell onto the heap, disappearing into legs and arms of chairs, upturned table tops, broken electrical fans, splintered wooden planks, dirt mixed with split stones and shattered bricks.

The door opened in the north wing. Old Wang sauntered out. Li An quickly stepped outside.

"Have you had breakfast yet?" Li An greeted him.

"Yes, yes. Is your son coming tonight?" Old Wang asked. "I want to talk to him."

"Come over for dinner," Li An said. "Where are you off to now?"

"What're you cooking tonight?"

"Dumplings, of course."

"I must go to my daughter's now. My grandchild is almost due."

"I'll wait for you for dinner." Li An watched Old Wang walking slowly out the courtyard gate before returning to her room.

The room had hardly changed since the death of her husband. Their bed, pushed against the wall, was stacked with their wedding comforters, two big cedar trunks tucked neatly beneath the bed, covered with crocheted white lace. An old drafting table with shortened legs occupied the entire length of another wall. Clear glass covered the table top, under which were pictures of neighbors and friends collated with random notes, postcards, letters, business cards, newspaper clippings, magazine articles. On the wall above the table was a *Huang Li*, the Chinese daily calendar, displaying Sunday in big red characters with all the ferocity of alarm. Next to it a Gregorian calendar showed a traditional Chinese brush painting of chrysanthemums for the month of September. Each day past crossed out with a big X in ballpoint pen. The last row remained uncrossed. A dressing table, salvaged from a parting neighbor, was the only new addition after her son had moved out; it sat where his cot once was.

Opening the bottom drawer of the dresser, Li An paused, then selected an aubergine-colored western-style jacket to put it on over her gray sweater. From under layers of neatly folded clothes her hands found the *zi tan* wooden jewelry box. Carefully she placed it on top of the dresser and examined her face in the mirror, her index finger tracing her eyebrows. A few strands of newly waved hair flipped out, she tugged them behind her ears. Opening the *zi tan* box, she picked out a pair of small golden earrings and threaded them carefully into each of her earlobes, avoided looking at the black-and-white wedding photo glued to the inside of the box. She closed the box and put it back underneath all the clothes. At last, she changed into freshly polished leather pumps. The young man on the phone had insisted that she should not be late, and gave her detailed directions. Before leaving her room, Li An took off the golden earrings and returned them to the *zi tan* box. The apartment buildings, the young man said, were outside the Sixth Ring Road.

Li An sat high up by the window on a crowded bus leaving the city. She watched young men and women in pairs, silently murmuring to each other.

The day her husband did not come home was a fine spring day. As usual, he had gotten on his bicycle in the morning and waved good-bye to go to work. Their son was barely a year old. It was *Qing Ming*, time for the annual content switching of the cedar trunks: storing the winter clothes and shaking out the spring ones. Li An had waited for him to come home till the moon was high.

He had passed *Tian An Men Square* at the wrong time of day by mistake, said the head of the neighborhood association. It was a shame. He was such a fine person, young with a beautiful wife and a newborn, caught up in the spring protest of the Gang of Four.

Li An was stunned and silent.

Old Wang's wife and others from the courtyard took turns staying with her. They looked after her son until it was winter time, until she regained the ability to cry, until everyone had exhausted stories of relatives and friends going to the countryside and not coming back, of years spent in prison not knowing one's best friend was in the next cell, of missed losses one didn't even know about, like the man who came out of prison to learn he had shrunk five centimeters. "Life is such," Old Wang comforted her. "Don't kill it with your pain." But Li An felt irritated and angry at her infant son's cry, his neediness for her bosoms, and his face with his father's eyes, nose, and that high forehead. She began marking an X for each day that passed on the calendar.

She gazed out the bus window. An old man in a drab winter jacket and skewed baseball hat pulled a three-wheeled cart piled high with cardboard boxes, grinning for no apparent reason. A kiosk girl stood rearranging magazines and newspapers. A young man on a moped zipped next to the bus, cigarette dangling from his mouth. He shouted into his cell phone while spitting in the street. A colorful spandex-clad racing bicyclist with a red helmet thrust upon the moped, stopping a hair behind its rear wheel. The light changed. With a scream the moped sped up, leaving a thin tube of black smoke in the air. Li An watched the bicyclist raising himself above the seat, pedaling rapidly, quickly overtaking the moped. His red helmet threaded through traffic like a colorful snake. The bus headed north towards the mountain, moving farther away from the city center. The fog thinned.

As the slim, clean-shaven city youths left the bus, a crowd of sturdy country folks boarded, carrying on their backs dull blue cloth bags bursting at seams. They shouted at each other as they stacked their bags together, and laughed when the bus jerked forward and one man fell on top. A laugh escaped from Li An, but she quickly turned away, ashamed of her gleefulness. At the next stop, a group of young women in tight jeans came on, followed by a few young men with apple-red cheeks, bright eyes, and thick black hair. There was hardly any standing room left on the bus. A young woman situated herself next to Li An, hooking her hand on the handlebar overhead. Her elbow swung near Li An's head. As the bus swirled, that elbow threatened to smash into Li An's forehead.

The road had widened. There were fewer pedestrians, bicyclists, and vehicles, more trucks. The sun climbed up in the sky, slanted into Li An's eyes. By the roadside, large patches of empty clearings alternated with vacant, newly constructed apartment blocks, waiting for someone like herself to come and buy. She remembered the orchards and vegetable fields that once extended to the mountain's base. Her family, unlike her husband's, was an old Beijing family. Her grandmother had had bound feet, and told stories of ghosts, lamented the fall of the city wall and the burial of the imperial moat.

The bus followed the Grand Canal north, diverting

occasionally to circle small towns at its edge. Finally, it stopped and emptied all its passengers onto a street without sidewalks. She remembered the young man's instruction: take the bus to the end of the line, go north for 500 meters, then walk eastward for another 200 meters, the buildings would be new with blue glass.

A young man in a bright red jacket stood at the sidewalk-to-be. "Ms. Li, welcome!" he said. "Please come with me." When he raised one hand to wave at her, his jacket fluffed like a flapping red flag in light wind. His other hand held a phone into which he shouted, "Ms. Li just arrived."

Another young man rushed out of the blue glass building holding a yellow hardhat, handing it to Li An. Li An stared at the hat, puzzled until she saw the young man gesturing, "Put it on please." He led her through a lobby under construction, into an elevator of mirrors that ascended slowly all the way to the top floor. Three more smiling young men in red suits greeted her in unison when the elevator door opened, "Ms. Li, welcome!"

"Please sign in, Ms. Li," one said, thrusting a clipboard and pen into Li An's hand and helping her take off the hardhat.

"Did you have a good trip?" another asked.

"Did you bring your cell phone?" the third one said.

"Of course," she said. "My son insisted."

"Please turn it off, Ms. Li, while you are meeting with our manager," the third young man said. He waited until she found her phone and turned it off before leading her down the carpeted hallway to an apartment.

A rush of deafening noise poured out to greet her.

The apartment burned with blinding brightness and was filled with small round tables, each manned by a young man in a red suit. She was led to one.

"Ms. Li, how are you today?" Her young man was very tall and thin, like a sapling. His face was full of zits, one so prominent it sat right on the tip of his nose. Li An couldn't take her eyes off it. She thought it might explode anytime.

"I'm good …"

"Sit down, sit down. Thank you for taking the time to come out here, Auntie Li. *A yi*, do you take vacations?"

"Vacation …"

"Do you dream of the American West?"

"Where …"

Her young man shouted above the clamor inside the apartment, "The stress of modern life – the noise, the overcrowding, the traffic, the pollution, the lightning pace…" with each phrase, he raised his right arm high above his head, before letting gravity pull it down to his thigh, making a soft slapping sound that was lost to all except Li An, "…is great. Take family and friends to a remote part of Inner Mongolia, to ride horses on the vast, empty grassland, to experience nature, to BBQ by bonfire at night, to…"

"Inner Mongolia? I only want to buy an apartment big enough for my son, so we can all live together, closer to each…"

"Please, *a yi*, let me finish my pitch…" the young man leaned forward. Li An looked away, ashamed at her interruption. The young man raised his arm again, and quickly found his way back to the perfectly pitched rhythm.

"…our big boss will give you, Ms. Li, a free ticket to fly to Inner Mongolia to spend a weekend there. For free!" His hand rested on his thigh.

Li An's eyes wandered to the young woman at the next table. She wore a white scarf covering her head and had a heart-shaped mouth. Li An felt thirsty.

"I'm so sorry, but can I have some water?" she requested.

Her young man sighed, waved his arm high into the air as if to call an army into action. A young woman in a blue jacket rushed over.

"Xiao Liu, get auntie some water." He turned back to Li An and began once more without a pause, "Ms. Li, would you be interested in purchasing a house?"

"Where is the house?"

"Let me show you a map." Her young man raised his arm once more, waved, called out, "Xiao Liu, get me the map!"

The same young woman rushed back to them with a binder, opening it to reveal a well-thumbed map.

"Water," Li An said.

"Xiao Liu, quickly! Where is the water? *A yi* is thirsty." Her young man looked as if he also needed a drink of water. "If you make a small deposit today, Ms. Li, we can guarantee a discount of twenty percent off the advertised price."

"But I don't want a house in Inner Mongolia. I just want an inexpensive apartment in Beijing," Li An said. "I should leave."

"Please, *a yi*, please let me finish my routine," her young man begged, raising his arm above his head again as if to draw an exclamation mark.

Li An looked away toward the young woman with the scarf and focused her eyes on her heart-shaped mouth. She desperately needed a drink of water. She inhaled deeply and fell back into her chair as it tipped under her weight: light and life appeared on layers of a wedding cake as in a movie. She saw the Double Happiness signs on the windowpanes, her husband with a big red paper flower on his left breast against the deep blue worker's jacket; she saw the parades of cheering crowds marching through their *hu tong* in front of their courtyard gate; she saw broken glass, fallen tree branches and smashed bricks scattered in the courtyard, the mouth of a bawling little boy, the piercing screams that broke the eardrums, a face of tiny red dots and a pale hand fanning above her face, the heart-shaped mouth, and a soft voice called out, "*A yi, a yi*, wake up, wake up." She felt screaming hot and thirsty.

"Oh I'm all right, I'm all right." Li An tried to sit up. The young woman with the scarf held her gently and stroked her arm, as Li An drank greedily from a cup of water handed to her by the young man with zits. Quietly her young man sat with both hands resting on the thighs, and watched Li An, until she got up and left alone.

Outside the building, Li An stood, a little lost, by the wide boulevard without sidewalks, waiting for a break in the ceaseless parade of vehicles to cross the street. She leaned on a newly planted sapling, watching an ingenious farmer spreading grain on the boulevard to dry; a swarm of bicyclists passed by. Seizing a break in the traffic, she ran across, headed toward the bus stop. The young woman with heart-shaped mouth was there too. Li An bowed slightly, feeling embarrassed. Together, they waited for the bus in silence. The spandex-clad bicyclist flew by. The air stirred, then swirled. Both women looked and smiled at each other.

"*A yi*, let me accompany you home," the young woman with the heart-shaped mouth said shyly.

"It's cold," Li An said, stamping her feet on the

ground, stirring up dust that settled on her once-polished shoes. She fingered a movie ticket in her pocket and remembered the last time she had worn the jacket was when she had gone to watch a movie made by her son. "It will be too much trouble for you."

"Oh, no, not at all. I live near *Niu Jie*. Where do you live, *a yi*?"

"I live near *Gu Lou*."

"We are heading in the same direction."

During the long bus ride back to the city center, both women fell silent. The movie her son had made played in Li An's mind. There was so much violence, blood, and discontent. She doubted his father would have liked it.

Arriving at Li An's bus stop, she asked the young woman, "Please come and stay for dinner. I'm making fennel and pork dumplings tonight."

"*A yi*, that's so nice of you, but, I'm a *Hui Min*." The young woman smiled.

"You are a Muslim. I can make other fillings too. Please come."

"I should go home. My parents and others are waiting for me." The young woman left her name and phone number with Li An and promised she would come to visit her soon.

Walking home from the bus stop, Li An was stopped by the American woman who had bought the adjacent courtyard. She waved to Li An, "Auntie, *a yi*, please visit. Come inside." Li An laughed at the American's stilted Mandarin, and felt curiously pulled by this foreigner's desire for companionship. Stepping into the American's courtyard, she was transported. But the colors were all wrong: the eaves were painted steel blue, the columns brown, and the doors light beige. She was impressed with the brick-paved garden, the shrubs and trees, and the brightly painted red corridor ceilings along the east and west wings with stenciled scenes from *A Dream of Red Mansions*. There was no clutter and no junk, nothing astray. The doors of the north main receiving hall were open. Li An peeked inside at the stately Ming and Qing antiques, the solemn wall with the ancestry scroll painting, and felt she was in a museum: distant, untouchable, pristine, reticent. She turned quickly and said she needed to go home to cook.

Back in her room, she waited for Old Wang as she sat on a stool, hunched over the little round chopping board, mixing the flour, chopping the meat. Outside the courtyard came the cry of the junk collector accompanied by a faint, crisp jingle. Li An stopped to put on a pair of tattered gloves, and walked up to the foot of the persimmon tree, studying the pile. Carefully she tugged on a protruding leg. It wouldn't budge. Li An stood back. The cry of the junk collector was approaching. She repositioned her legs in a *tai chi* pose, and with a sudden pull, a sun-faded seat of a chair emerged from the debris. Just then, another pair of hands slid in beside hers, grabbing the other leg. Shoulder to shoulder they pulled – one, two, three – and a two-legged chair surfaced. Li An turned to thank her helper, a disheveled man with a big grin who smelled of alcohol. Together they pulled out a tabletop, an old hair dryer, a broken mirror, small planks of wood, another broken chair, a bottomless pot. They carried all into the *hu tong*, and piled them onto the junk cart.

"Have you eaten?" Li An turned to her helper. "Stay for some dumplings. I make the best in this entire *hu tong*."

"Next time. Next time." The helper turned to assist others who had come out of their homes with pieces of broken furniture and appliances. The junk collector pressed a fistful of loose change into Li An's hand. Laughter and chatter filled the usually quiet alley, the *hu tong* became congested, an obstacle course for the spandex-clad racing bicyclist who entered from the far end, coming toward them. Li An held her breath as she watched the cyclist maneuvering around people, junk, and cart, disappearing into a bend in the *hu tong.* She waved as the junk collector left with his helper, then went back to her room and apportioned loose change into the jars that lined her windowsill.

That evening, Li An's son did not come for dinner. Old Wang and Li An finished all the dumplings.

"We two are the only ones left from this courtyard." Old Wang said. "Not many old houses are left on the street. Most are gone."

"Are you thinking … wonder if it's a boy or girl?"

"I hope it's a granddaughter. Her *lao wai* husband from France, you never know."

"Yes. A daughter is much better to have, closer to home. It's been five years since your wife passed away."

"I'm old now, full of fears, especially this fear of losses. No beginnings without endings. What should I embrace, fear or loss? What do you think? *Xiao Li*?"

Li An thought about her husband, her son. She quietly listened as Old Wang continued. "Since my wife died, I have not lived. Thinking of my future grandchild, I decided to try facing losses for a change." With that, Old Wang went on to talk more about his daughter and son-in-law. He said he would begin taking French lessons.

That night a rare autumn rain fell in Beijing. Li An lay awake, listening to the pitter-patter of the raindrops, and thought about her own fears and losses. She suddenly remembered she would be sixty this year, Old Wang was almost seventy, her husband who had died thirty-three years earlier would have been sixty-five, and she had forgotten to cross the day that had just passed with an X.

In the morning, she got up early and boiled water for tea. Standing at her windowsill, she watched the door of the north wing, waiting for it to open. Suddenly she turned and took out the little *zi tan* jewelry box from the dresser. She studied the wedding photo glued inside and picked out the golden earrings, threading each stud into her earlobes. She would tell Old Wang she too could learn French.

Teresa Stenson

Blue Raincoat

The last thing she gave you, the last time you saw her, the last thing you talked about.

'All the lasts,' you say.

I tell you not to wear it. 'It doesn't mean anything. You know what's important – '

Nothing sounds right. How can I know? I know you don't like it, it rests awkwardly, doesn't fit. You are earth, the raincoat is sky. Sky blue, big buttoned, double lapelled, wide at the bottom. You stare at your reflection and I stand a metre away, not knowing how to come closer.

We were here by the hallway mirror three months ago when you brought it home. 'It's so wide. Swing-style, apparently. Makes me look pregnant,' you shot a look at me, 'but I'm not.'

I wouldn't have minded if you were. But I didn't say that. 'It's "try-hard",' you said, 'like it's trying to be a raincoat with bells on.' We laughed a bit, but I knew it stood for more when you asked your reflection, 'She's my mother. How could she not know I'd *hate* this?'

That day it didn't matter if my words weren't right, because I moved to you and slid it off your shoulders, pulled the sleeves, let it fall from you. Said I'd take it to a charity shop if you wanted.

'No. Maybe. She might visit and wonder where it is. Leave it a while.'

So it stayed buried in its bag in the small and low cupboard underneath the coat hooks that were covered in your browns; long scarves trailing to the floor like roots.

Until today. 'I want to wear it.'

'It's just – today, Luce, it might look –'

'I don't care. I'll tell them she gave it to me. It'll cheer everyone up.'

'It's quite warm, really warm, you might feel –'

'I'll feel fine.'

*

Between your sisters you are small, anchored and choked by the raincoat. You match the sky but face the ground, shoulders showing me your short quick breaths. The top button of the coat is pressed against your throat. Such little air flows into and out of you.

You told me once, 'There are no spaces inside of us. When you open a human body it's packed dense, not like the diagrams showing light pink spaces around everything, it's not like that. All the organs fit in and around each other, with no room for anything else.'

And now your heavy no-space-no-air insides are all I can think about, and how I want to rush over to you, open the coat, and let air fill the life pipes all leading their way in and out of you.

*

The buttons hang by just a few strands of cotton, the cuffs turn brown. You do not 'swing'. I find you at the hallway mirror.

'It's been four weeks, Lucy.' I say it like it's important, but I just want you to see, make you better. I move over, and you let me reach for a button, undo it. But then you jerk your arms up: 'No.'

The button comes off easily in my hand. There is a silence where your eyes turn down, your lips purse together, and you lower your arms to your side. You let me think your resolve is breaking, let me undo the other two buttons, ease the coat from your shoulders and let it fall. It is the closest we have felt for a long time. But you take a sharp breath at your reflection, and walk out the front door.

*

I wait for you. Give you time. It's summer and the night is still light, you are walking, breathing, letting air in. I know you will come through the door soon.

I have filled the sink with warm water and soap powder. Soaked, washed and spun your raincoat. Sewn the button back on, strengthened the others.

It hangs on the line.

You will come home soon, and I will scoop you up, you and your grief. I'll stay up all night listening, remembering everything about her with you. We will both laugh and we will both cry. You'll decide what to do with the raincoat: let's set it free. Tie string to it, make it a kite, let it fly.

I'll hold you until you fall asleep and in the morning you will smile and it will be another day, an easier day for us both doing things right and knowing how things are done.

I wait for you. Give you time.

But you don't come, and time without you slows and thickens, makes me work hard to pass through it. Time becomes segmented. Each piece is made from a question: how long have you been gone? how far away is her grave? how long would it take you to get there and back? how long has it been dark? how long should I wait? There is an equation in there somewhere, an adding up and taking away that will tell me what to do.

I want you to walk through the door. I want that sound – the click, swoosh: you have come back to me.

I want you to scoop me up, listen to my grief, let me be selfish, let me remember you. Spend a night laughing, crying, deciding. 'It's been hard for you,' you will say. 'But it's all okay now. It was just the raincoat. It is sky, and I'm earth.' And you'll hold me, and I'll feel your body, rub over your skin and it'll flake a little like dry mud, and I'll say, 'Yes, you are earth.' I'll let water stream onto you, and you will brighten.

You don't come.

*

I wear the raincoat, my arms bulging in the sleeves. It tears across the shoulders. In the hallway mirror, 'All the lasts,' I say.

I go to the graveyard. If you saw me here in this, would you come? But you are not here. I look for clues of you. Lay on the ground next to your Mum's headstone, run my hands over the grass, separate it and seek out the soil, push my fingers in. Cold, easy relief.

My eyes close under the weight of the sky and I wonder which bit of sky you are under. When they open and I lift my head everything looks muted. My eyes have forgotten every other colour but blue. I wait, let the world come back.

When I stand, I take the raincoat off. Lay it flat on the ground, fasten the buttons, smooth it down. From the waist, it fans out. I take the stones from my bag and place two in the bottom corners, one on each sleeve, one at the collar. I use more, the smaller stones and pebbles, until I have filled its outline. I leave it there: a flag, a surrender, a sign, a letter to you.

Nemone Thornes

Dancing with the Flag Man

A run of open-tread steps led to the caravan site's shop; a dark wooden building on tubular metal stilts. They reminded Elizabeth of the legs of a pier. As she and Chantelle approached it, two boys came through the door, followed by a furious-looking middle-aged man.

"Get out and stay out! You're banned for the rest of the week – and if there's any more nonsense, you're banned for life."

When they reached ground level one of the boys spat and the other turned around and looked up at the man.

This boy was different. He was about sixteen or seventeen, but his skin was as pale and perfect as that of a young child in a sentimental Victorian painting. The loose curls of brown silk hair reached to his shoulders.

"Wow!" Chantelle whispered. "He's even more gorgeous than David Cassidy."

"He's beautiful." Elizabeth said this partly for the sake of saying the right thing, and partly because it was true.

He kept on staring at the shop-man. The high-pitched barks of a dog filled the silence. The boy looked like an angry prince; his contempt was that of someone so far above the common people that it barely changed his exquisite face, but it was recognisable as contempt nonetheless. Eventually, he turned away and followed the other boy down the path.

Elizabeth remembered Chantelle's bedroom when her crush on David Cassidy was at its desperate, obsessive, hopeless height. Chan's room made you believe that they sold David Cassidy wallpaper. He wasn't in the charts very much now, and knowing that she hadn't forgotten him gave Elizabeth a warm feeling towards her. Perhaps her cousin was the loyal type.

They continued along the wide tarmac path. It was lined with caravans on both sides, and there were many more down narrower grassy side-roads. The caravans came in several sizes, but they were all white, and they all had an orange stripe running horizontally around them.

The sky was pale grey, a grey with a suggestion of brightness behind it: summer hidden by dirty net curtains. A breeze of neutral temperature blew through the site, through and over all the many metal objects – the cars, washing-line poles, picnic tables and the caravans themselves. It made a faint singing noise. The dog still barked.

It felt odd to be out in public in a dressing-gown, even though it was what everyone did: as Chantelle had said, there was no point in getting dressed just to go to the showers and get undressed again. Elizabeth hadn't liked the showers – there wasn't a lot of privacy in there. She kept her arms folded over her almost flat candlewick chest and wondered how Chantelle could feel comfortable wearing thin satin that ended at mid-thigh. Chan's breasts had grown a lot in the six months since Elizabeth had last seen her. Now they were bigger than many adult breasts, and they bounced as she walked. Chan was quite large all over now; she was starting to take after her mum, Elizabeth's Auntie Janice.

They reached the dog. It barked frantically and strained towards them, pulling at the lead that tied it to the steps of its owner's caravan. It was small, tan-coloured and very pretty, with a delicate pointed muzzle, black button eyes, and a tail like a fluffy question-mark. The noise had followed them all the way up to the shower-block, and all the way back down. It had been the last thing Elizabeth heard before she went to sleep and the first when she awoke. Last night, all the time they were unloading the car and for ages afterwards, it had barked constantly.

"It was like this in June," Auntie Janice had said. "Yap, yap, yap, all ruddy day. If it keeps on this time, I might ask to move."

They arrived back at Janice's caravan and found her sitting outside in a camping chair. Earlier, in ankle-length pink nylon, she had looked like a giant uncooked sausage. Now dressed, she was no longer sausage-shaped and she had a waist again. Elizabeth realised that her aunt must take her figure off and put it over a chair at night.

Janice's feet were up on a stool, and on a folding table at her side were her Embassy Regals, a *Daily Mirror*, a cup of tea and a radio from which Tom Jones was singing very loudly.

"I'm trying to drown it out," she said, meaning the barking. She reached down for her handbag, and gave Chantelle money "for the day."

Auntie Janice wasn't going out with them. It felt wrong – this wasn't what holidays were supposed to be like. If she were with her parents and her sister, they would all go somewhere together. When Elizabeth's father had proposed Janice's caravan, her sister had looked as if she were being offered a fortnight's oakum-picking, and had arranged to stay with a friend.

They went inside to dress, then Chantelle led Elizabeth through the caravans to a wide, flat cliff-top. Once out of the site, the breeze was stronger. This was a sea breeze with ambition, Elizabeth thought. It was determined to work very hard, pass all its exams, and become a proper wind eventually. The uniform grey cloud had now cleared a little in places, and the sky looked like torn fabric with pale blue showing beneath the damage. There was weak, unambitious sunshine; the sort that never did its homework and would amount to nothing.

They walked along the edge of the cliff. The grey-blue sea, touched with white foam, was an eiderdown from which the feathers were escaping. Under it, someone gently snored, making the feathers rise and fall. She imagined Chan's face if she said that the breeze was working on its exams, and the sea looked like an eiderdown. All the most interesting thoughts Elizabeth had were things that you couldn't say out loud.

A set of metal steps led down to the seafront, where a row of beach-huts sat at the edge of the sand. One of them was covered in coloured bunting, long strings of it that ran all the way from the apex of the roof down to the ground. It was exactly like the bunting strung between the lamp posts in Elizabeth's street, when there had been an outdoor party for the Queen's Silver Jubilee the previous year.

"That's the local loony's hut," said Chan. "He lives in it. He wanders around pushing a pram, and he's got those little flag things sewn all over his clothes, too."

Elizabeth crossed the road and went to the front of the hut. There was a deck-chair on the veranda, and the chair was also covered in bunting. The roof of the hut was yellow, the walls were red, the door was green and there were white curtains, held back with big, bright blue bows. On the window ledge was a vase of plastic roses. It looked very appealing, like something from a children's picture-book. Elizabeth didn't say this out loud, either. Chantelle got funny if you had the wrong opinions about things.

They walked on. When they reached the harbour, Chan said, "Well, this is it." She gestured towards the cafés and amusement arcades on the esplanade. "I wanted mum to get a van at Blackpool, but she wouldn't. It was all right here at first, but it's a bit boring now."

A little while later Chantelle saw something that interested her very much indeed: the two boys from the shop were sitting in the long window of the ice-cream parlour. Soon, Elizabeth found that she was sitting in the same window, but unfortunately for Chan, the only free table was some distance from the boys.

Chantelle sat very straight and ate very slowly. Every so often she brushed her hair back from her face and gave her head a little shake. Suddenly, she looked distressed.

"Damn! They're going." She got up. Elizabeth stayed at the table and watched her catch up with them. They stood on the pavement outside the window while Chan talked to the boy who wasn't beautiful. The beautiful one didn't speak, but he stared at Elizabeth until she looked away.

Chan bounced back onto her chair. "They're brothers. You wouldn't guess, would you? The gorgeous one must be really stuck-up – he just looked at me like I was dirt. The other one's nice; he's called Darren. Their parents have just bought a Permanent on the site. He said they'd probably go to the arcades later."

After the ice-cream breakfast, Chantelle went immediately to one of the arcades, but a few minutes later she said they had better try a different one. This proved to be the pattern of the day. Elizabeth was surprised: how could Chantelle actually want to spend so much time doing something so dull? How could she bear it? She had never realised before that boredom could be almost a physical thing – if it went on too long, it was a sort of torture. There was a brief escape at lunchtime, to sit on the harbour wall and eat chips, then Chantelle insisted on going back inside. She wasn't even really interested in the actual machines.

Chantelle had just turned sixteen. Elizabeth wondered if this was what was in store for her when she was as old as Chan – would she become so obsessed with boys? Was that what happened to everybody?

Later, a whole lifetime later, as they walked back along the cliff-top to the caravan, Elizabeth heard faint wind-blown music. They gained on the sound, which turned out to be coming from a man with a pram.

"Told you we'd see the nutter. He wanders about with that thing all the time. He's touched." Chan tapped her head.

Soon they overtook him. He wore a black suit, and fluttering from it, sewn in rows on the back of the jacket and down the arms and legs were triangles of coloured fabric – red, green, yellow, white and blue.

His pram was big and black and its full curves were outlined in chrome. It looked solid and heavy, like a grand old car. The wheels were bigger than those of most bicycles. The hood was folded flat, and a dark wooden board filled the space where a baby should have been. A wind-up gramophone sat on top of the board. Under the hiss and crackle of the record you could hear the machine working. It sounded as if there were a tiny steam engine in there.

It didn't look like Elizabeth's idea of a gramophone; they had big foxglove-flower horns, but this one was just a box. She wanted to ask where the sound was coming from. It was loud, even without a horn. She had never heard music quite like it. There were no drums, but it did have a beat, and it was compelling in just the same way that pop was compelling. A man with a posh, old-fashioned voice was singing about being in love, but he sounded tremendously…jolly about it. Jolly. Yes.

That was the right word. A strictly regimented army of strings and horns marched under him. The army's purpose was to provide as much fun and happiness as possible.

Elizabeth looked back. The man smiled. She smiled. She stopped and the man stopped too. Chantelle went on.

He had a plastic rose where other people might have a bow-tie. Apart from being covered in bunting flags, his suit was neat and new-looking – and expensive, too, she thought; like something a rich person would wear. There was nothing off-putting about his appearance: he was slim and clean-shaven, and he wasn't all that old; probably a bit older than her father.

He swayed his body and moved his hands. Elizabeth understood.

"Yes. Makes you feel like dancing."

His smile broke into a big grin. Out of her eye corner she saw Chantelle turn around. The record reached its end and clicked, clicked, clicked. The flag man lifted the playing arm from the record and pushed a little lever at the side of the turntable. There was a long metallic squeal and the record stopped moving. Chantelle reached them, scowling, and hooked her arm through Elizabeth's.

"Come *on*." She pulled hard, almost making Elizabeth lose her balance, and set off back the way she had come, taking Elizabeth with her. "What are you *doing*? You don't *talk* to him."

Elizabeth looked back and smiled at the flag man again. He smiled and raised his hand. A tiny wave.

"Chantelle! There's no need to be rude!" She said it loudly, because he was still in earshot.

"He's cuckoo. Nuts. You can *see* that. Why did you *stop*?"

"I liked the music."

Chantelle laughed, unpleasantly. "You're as bonkers as he is." She dropped Elizabeth's arm. Behind them, another song began, as compelling as the first. It made Elizabeth want to dance along the cliff-top. She could see herself leaping and twirling, feel herself being carried along by that jolly army. There were more interesting ways of getting to places than mere walking – you could dance there, if you had the right music.

Back at the caravan, Auntie Janice had a bright, shiny going-out dress on, and her hair was in Carmen rollers.

"I'll be ready in two ticks, then I'll take you up to the cafeteria."

"Perhaps they'll be there," said Chantelle, once Janice had returned to her preparations.

Janice bought meals that came with two kinds of vegetables, and she wanted to know how Chantelle and Elizabeth had spent their time. It was obviously adult responsibility hour. As she listened to Chantelle's account, Elizabeth discovered that as well as pretending to play penny falls for several decades so Chan could watch out for two boys, they had done all sorts of other things. They had been on the beach, and to the park, and they had looked around the gift-shops, too. In fact, they hadn't been to the amusement arcades or met any boys at all. What a surprise, to find that the entire, awful day had never happened!

Responsibility hour over, Janice left them outside the cafeteria door with instructions to go straight back to the caravan, and to behave.

"Does your mum go out a lot?" Elizabeth asked, as they walked back through the site.

"She has done since Dad died." Chan giggled. "She wants to find a new man! She does find them sometimes, but they don't last."

They watched the black-and-white television. There was a subtitled film with lots of embarrassing scenes. Throughout the nudity and kissing and groaning, Chantelle speculated about Darren, and wondered how to meet him again. She seemed to have forgotten his beautiful brother.

Auntie Janice came in very late. Elizabeth, woken by the disturbance, realised why she needed to put her feet up all day. If you wanted to be kind about it, she thought, you could say that it was because her evenings were terribly tiring. She was so completely worn out that she was finding it very difficult to get ready for bed. The process involved an awful lot of crashing around. At one point, it sounded as though she had fallen over from sheer exhaustion. Elizabeth wondered if Auntie Janice often got so drunk, and remembered her mother's doubts about placing her in Janice's care. Her father had said, "Oh, come on. She's not as bad as all that." Elizabeth's parents had won a Mediterranean cruise – a cruise just for two – in a prize draw, and this had caused a strange alteration in her father's opinions about his sister.

Elizabeth didn't sleep again for a long time. The only noises to break the late-night silence were Janice's snores and the occasional barking of the small dog.

In the morning Elizabeth woke to a woman's screaming. Then there was a desperate keening sound. She looked across the narrow gap between the beds and met Chantelle's wide eyes. Elizabeth and Chantelle got up. Auntie Janice's bedroom door opened at the same moment as theirs. They followed Janice outside, and up the main path. Other people were hurrying in the same direction.

A middle-aged woman sat on the steps of the barking dog's caravan. She had stopped making howling noises, and was just crying noisily. Another woman was crouching down next to the steps with her arm around her.

The weeping woman clutched something to her chest. It was the colour of the barking dog. The woman's dressing-gown was smeared and splashed with red.

"He came back to me to die!" she shouted, eventually, to the small crowd that had gathered. "I'd just come out and he wasn't here and I was going to look for him, and then he came running and as soon as he saw me he dropped dead. I don't know how he managed to get here, with what they'd done to him." Then she crumpled like a popped balloon, her head dropped to her knees and she wept again.

The woman comforting her looked up and said, "They cut his throat. And they cut his tail off."

Everyone started talking. Janice turned away, and motioned Elizabeth and Chantelle to retreat.

"Come on. I'll go and see her later, when she's got over the shock a bit." Auntie Janice walked in silence for a few moments. "How could anyone *do* that? I mean, it was a blasted nuisance with all that barking, but I wouldn't have wished that on the poor little thing."

They returned to the caravan. Janice made tea, and wondered aloud what the world was coming to. Eventually, Elizabeth and Chantelle set off for the town.

Out on the cliff-top, they saw another dog. It lay on its side, not moving.

Chantelle shouted, "Oh no – look!" and they ran to it.

"Is it...still alive?"

"No..." said Chan, uncertainly.

Elizabeth made herself look closely. The dog definitely wasn't breathing.

"No. No, it isn't."

Chantelle's hands covered her mouth. She made little panicky whimpering noises. "Oh God, it's awful! What's going on?" Elizabeth put her arm around her and Chan clutched her hand.

It was a medium-sized dog, a dull black mongrel, and it was covered in blood. There was blood on the grass all around it, especially near its neck. A red-black line about an inch wide ringed its throat. A wave of nausea washed through Elizabeth. Her eyes flinched away and met the dog's eyes, which were filmed over.

"What happened to it?" Chan said.

"The same as the other one, I think. Someone cut its throat."

"Yeah, you're right. It's totally sick!"

"Totally. It's scary."

"One was bad enough, but this is horrible." Chan shuddered. "Horrible."

"Do you think we ought do something?"

"Like what? Bury it?"

"Tell someone, I mean."

"Oh – yeah. Let's go back and tell mum."

Auntie Janice was appalled, and set off for the site office. Chantelle and Elizabeth returned to the cliffs, and approached the steps to the seafront by a dog-avoiding route. When they came to the flag man's hut, Chantelle stopped.

"He did it!" she said. She sounded surprised, as though she'd had a moment of inspiration about a complex problem which she had spent the morning trying to work out.

"The flag man? Why would he do it?"

"Stands to reason, dunnit? He's the local loony."

She nodded towards the hut. "It's probably full of dead dogs."

By the late morning, back inside one of the amusement arcades, Elizabeth realised that the phrase 'to die of boredom' wasn't just an expression that people used. It would actually happen to her if she had to watch one more row of fruit failing to line up.

"They'll probably never come, and we'll have wasted the whole day."

"Let's just give it another hour."

"I'm really sorry Chantelle, but I don't think I can stand it for another hour." She made a decision. Rather, the decision made itself – she had to get away. "I'm going. Come on – come with me. Let's do something else for a while. We can come back later."

Chantelle refused. What did that say? That she had no powers of leadership at all?

She walked out into the sunshine. This was a sun that got triple As and gold stars on all its homework. She would, finally, explore the town, even if she had to do it on her own.

Several hours of exploration later, in the seafront park, she saw the flag man. The song floating from the big black pram seemed like the musical equivalent of the weather. All day, memories of the dogs had kept jumping back into her mind, but with the music, the dogs faded a little. Another old-fashioned voice sang, a female one this time, and her tired feet suddenly wanted to dance.

The flag man noticed her and waved. They walked towards each other.

"Hello," said Elizabeth. He smiled, pulled a small white card from his pocket and handed it to her.

Sadly, I'm physically unable to speak – but the music speaks for me!

"Oh. I was going to ask you something." He made a face which said, very clearly, "What?"

"How does your gramophone work? It hasn't got a horn. Where does the sound come from?"

He pointed into an opening at one corner of the machine, then gestured over it, using both hands to form the shape of a funnel. Elizabeth understood.

"It does have a horn, but the horn's inside the box?"

He nodded, and took a notebook from another pocket.

Three girls of about her own age passed close by, looked over their shoulders, turned back to each other and started laughing.

The flag man handed her the notebook. It said, in elegant slanted handwriting: *It's a portable gramophone. The ones with the big horns were for in your house.*

The record came to its end, and Elizabeth saw Darren's beautiful brother walking towards them. He was unmistakable, even at a distance. She couldn't, couldn't, couldn't be seen talking to the flag man by Darren's brother.

"I've got to go now. I love your music. Thank you."

She walked away as quickly as she could without breaking into a run. Poor Chantelle, she thought. If she had only known.

Darren's brother caught up with her at the park gates.

"Hi. I saw you yesterday, with that other girl. You're staying at the caravan dump too, yeah?"

"Um…yeah."

He was talking to her. To her. It was like meeting a film star – well, like she imagined that would be.

"I'm Jon. Without an 'h'. Jay-oh-en."

"Hello."

"What's your name?"

"Elizabeth."

"Hiya, Liz." It was always disappointing when people shortened her name. She liked to be 'Elizabeth', but no one ever said it in full, apart from her parents. At least 'Liz' was an improvement on 'Bet'.

Jon asked more questions – about how long she was staying; where she lived; if Chantelle was her sister. Elizabeth thought her answers sounded boring, and felt the heat of embarrassment spreading over her cheeks. Soon, Jon winked, said "See ya," and ran off back into the park.

With a sense of failure, Elizabeth walked out onto the esplanade. It wouldn't have made any difference if she had been able to think of some worthwhile things to say, though. Someone as glamorous as Jon would never be really interested in her.

The murdered dog had been removed from the cliff-top. Inside the site, the barking dog's caravan was silent and the car that usually stood beside it had gone. The door was closed and the awning over it was folded away. There were splashes of dried blood all around the steps.

When Chantelle and Elizabeth arrived on the seafront the next morning, they saw that they had missed a dramatic event.

"Chantelle…look."

"Wow."

One beach-hut hardly existed any more. It was black. It no longer had a roof. The walls of the huts on either side were scarred with smoke.

"It's the flag man's."

"Yeah. Oh, well."

"He lived there!"

Elizabeth ran across the road. Chantelle followed more slowly to the front of the hut.

"Bet? What is it? What's the matter?"

"How can you say that?" Chantelle looked blank. "He lived here. Look at it – there's nothing left inside. It's just a shell. Suppose he was asleep? Suppose he's dead?"

"Oh, Bet, don't cry. He was only an old mental case."

"I'm going to look for him."

All that day, Elizabeth walked the town, hoping to see colours fluttering on a black suit. Chantelle had again refused to accompany her, and now probably thought she was quite mad.

Elizabeth walked, walked, walked. Eventually, back on the cliff-top, she saw a figure, a black figure. She ran. It was a black figure with some specks of colour…and the flag man had his pram. She ran as fast as she could and the music came to meet her.

He looked perfectly clean, neat and unharmed.

"I thought you might have died! In the fire. I'm so glad you're all right."

He smiled broadly, and took his notebook from his pocket.

I was at home.

"My cousin said you lived in the hut."

She watched him write. He wrote so quickly!

I live with my mother. She's not very well. She's old, I look after her. When you live with your mother, you need somewhere else to go sometimes – so I had the hut.

"I'm really sorry about that."

Thank you. So am I. On another line, he had added: *What's your name?*

"Elizabeth."

That's nice. It suits you.

He bent down to the records, which were in a box on a wire tray under the pram. Elizabeth looked at them, too: Jack Hylton; Ambrose and his Orchestra; The Savoy Orpheans.

"What's yours?"

He straightened up, gave her a record and reached for his notebook again.

William.

"Hello, William."

The record was *Henry's Made a Lady Out of Lizzie.* He gently took it back, and wound the handle of the gramophone. The song seemed to be about a car called Lizzie.

I'm sorry it's not Elizabeth, but it's the nearest I have.

"Thank you."

He held out his hands, inviting her to dance, but she shook her head.

"I love the record, though."

Elizabeth and William played the records and talked, in speech and handwriting, about the music. When people walked past they all looked back over their shoulders. The longer she stayed with him, the less she minded. Waiting for it was even quite funny. "I know what you're going to do now," she thought, as two middle-aged women approached.

By the time she left William she had made a great discovery: she deeply and passionately loved a singer called Al Bowlly. William thought Al Bowlly was a brilliant singer, too. He had said – written – that she had excellent taste.

Chantelle met a new boy at the fairground that evening. She didn't know him, but soon she was behaving as if they knew each other very well indeed. Elizabeth had her first experience of being a wallflower.

"I'm really tired," she said. "I think I'll go back now."

Chantelle said "Oh no, *don't*," but judging by the look on her face, Elizabeth didn't think she was too distressed about her departure.

She walked along the esplanade and climbed the metal steps to the cliff-top. The flamingo pink sunset had faded, and the sky was a peculiar deep violet. It made her think of horror stories, of the sort of people who come out only at night. The violet was darkening from the top, as if something huge and black were squashing the sky down into the sea. She imagined what would happen if there really were a huge mass hanging up there, forcing itself downwards. The sea would be pushed out of shape by the sky, it would rise up and roll, as if smooth-backed monsters undulated beneath the surface. Sometimes, in foreign countries, the sea really did rise up. Huge waves came out of nowhere and swamped the land. People died.

There was no one walking on the cliffs. Perhaps there were murderers hiding in the bushes, or enormous flightless moths and great black beetles shouldering their way through the undergrowth. She listened to the heavy breathing of waiting, watching maniacs and the rustling of giant, land-bound, lumbering insects.

Then there were real sounds: male voices. Two figures appeared in silhouette against the fading violet. Men, or boys. The head of a large dog showed in profile. The men, or boys, bent over it. Elizabeth froze. Whatever was happening wasn't good. The other dogs were still vivid in her mind. This dog yelped, twice. She crouched down on the springy grass. She made herself small. There was a smell, a smell like petrol, a whooshing sound, and where there had been a dog there was a fire. The fire jumped into the air – the dog's muzzle pointed straight up to the sky and its back streamed with flames. It squealed and yelped and squealed, and shot upwards three times. On the third jump the fire engulfed its head, then it no longer had a dog's shape, but was a ragged burning ball. Somewhere, somewhere more distant, the boys or men jeered and laughed.

Elizabeth's skin crawled and crackled. What must it be like to suffer so much pain? Tears poured from her but she didn't realise she was crying, and when she felt wetness on her face she had an instant of terror – she thought she was burning, too.

The dog ran. It looked like a mobile fire sweeping along the cliff, the flames flowing as if they were merely a long-haired dog's coat blown back by the wind of motion. The fireball grew smaller and the yelps and squeals fainter, then the fire vanished.

Elizabeth stayed where she was, crouched close to the grass. She listened. There were no male voices, only distant sounds from the town below and faint noises from the fairground. If they would do that to a dog, would they do it to a person, to a girl? Her heart was beating so fast that it hurt. She felt exposed, almost as if she were naked. The empty darkness all around her gave her the same sort of sensation that she imagined she would feel if the ground were not solid any more, and could drop away at any moment. Suppose they came back? Suppose she tried to get back to the caravan site, and she met them?

Elizabeth waited a long time before she thought it was safe to move.

In the morning, Chantelle went out with the new boy. The idea of going to the town alone was unappealing: it was frightening out there. All Elizabeth could think of was the burning dog. The images played and re-played in her mind, and tears tried to come. Auntie Janice had been horrified by the story, and when Elizabeth told her she would stay in the caravan and read, Janice said, "I don't blame you, lovey. I'm ashamed of this place now. It leaves a bad taste, doesn't it, this sort of thing? I might sell the van and get one in Blackpool after all – it's right put me off."

Later, Janice needed more Regals and asked Elizabeth to go to the shop. Outside one of the caravans near the shower-block, she saw Jon lying on a sun-lounger, eating crisps. He reminded her of a drawing in one of her History books, of rich Ancient Romans at a banquet. His crisps should have been figs in a golden bowl.

"Hiya, Liz."

A very short time later, Elizabeth climbed the steps to the shop on jellied legs. That evening, she would be going on a date. It was her first ever date, and it was with the most beautiful boy in the world. She supposed she would be safe from dog-murderers. Jon wouldn't let anything happen to her.

They left the fairground when the light was starting to fade. As they passed the burnt-out beach hut, Jon said, "I saw that go up. It went off like a bomb. Someone must've used petrol."

"It's awful. Poor man."

Jon laughed. "What – that old fruitcake? He's crazy. Totally barking mad."

"It was a horrible thing to do."

"He deserved it."

"Why?"

Jon laughed again. "He's stark staring bonkers. You don't behave the way he does unless there's something *seriously* wrong with you."

She wanted to argue, but that wouldn't make him like her. Jon didn't like her very much at all, she was sure he didn't. He was probably sorry he'd asked her out.

"I wonder who did it?" she said.

"Someone who hates loonies." Jon laughed yet again, but it wasn't funny; it was just cruel and pointless.

They walked to the lake in the park. The pedal-boats shaped like swans were resting at its edge. In the ash-grey light, their whiteness was somehow brighter and more startling than it was in the daytime. Giant yellow beaks loomed over Elizabeth's head.

"They don't tie them up. You can nick them." He grabbed the swan on the end of the row and pulled it around until it was side-on. "What you waiting for? Jump in."

"Someone will see. We'll get into trouble."

"Nah – it's fine. No one comes, this time of night."

She clambered over the wing and settled onto the far side of the bench. As Jon leapt in, the swan rocked, and water slapped against its sides. He sat down beside her and gave her a conspiratorial grin. She grinned back, and was conscious that it was the first moment of real connection in their entire evening.

They pedalled. The swan churned its way into the centre of the lake. Jon stopped pedalling. Elizabeth scanned the darkening park: there was no one around, so it was all right. For the moment.

Jon reached into his jacket, produced a full glass bottle, handed it to her: brandy.

"Well; have some." He lit another cigarette. She had already turned down so many that he had stopped offering.

"Um…OK." She unscrewed the bottle, sipped,

handed it back to him. Jon held it up to the remaining light.

"Call that a drink?" He took a swig, a big one. "How old are you, Liz?"

She wondered how big a lie she could tell, and decided to add on a whole year.

"Fifteen. Almost."

"You're only fourteen? You don't come across like fourteen. I reckoned you were sixteen, easy."

Elizabeth glowed, but the glow soon faded. Here she was, on a date with a wonderful, fabulous boy, but she wasn't having what she thought of as a good time. What was wrong with her? Other girls would kill to be in her place. The evening wasn't working and she didn't know why, but she had a feeling that the answer was there, just beyond reach, like a creature skulking in the shadows. If she could only have time to think she would be able to grab hold of it and drag it into the open. She felt she had been left behind by the runaway train of her own life. It was overwhelming to be with someone as special as Jon, and because it was overwhelming, she couldn't think properly.

The swan drifted. She asked which books he liked, but he just laughed. It pleased him if she drank the brandy, so she drank it. By the time they pedalled for the shore, she felt different: it didn't matter so much that she couldn't connect with Jon.

Back on the lakeside, he stood considering the swans.

"You could set fire to one."

"What?"

"You could. Fill it with stuff so it would really burn, really go up. Tie it to another one and tow it out, set fire to it and let it go, just push it away and leave it. It would look great – just imagine: one of these great big things out there, at night, all in flames."

It was the most animated he'd been, so far, and it sounded like a plan.

"You wouldn't though, would you?"

"Dunno. I might."

The skulking thought-creature slipped in and out of view at the corner of her mind's eye.

"Was it the beach hut that made you think of that?"

"Yeah. Must have been, mustn't it?" He laughed again. "Come on – I'm going to let you in on a secret."

They walked out of the park, along the sea-front, up the metal steps to the top of the cliff. The world was moving slightly and Elizabeth felt a little nauseous. Climbing the steps was difficult because they seemed to be not quite in the right places. Her feet clanged awkwardly down.

It was now fully dark. Well past the caravan site, Jon stopped. Square shapes loomed out of the bushes. Jon switched on a torch, led the way between two of the shapes, and pointed the torch at a padlock.

"Old lock-ups. Me and Darren found them. They're all empty, but I put a padlock on this one, so it could be my place. I kind of…got a house for free."

A free cliff hut, she thought, thinking of William.

Jon's torch showed that the lock-up was deeply ridged metal, painted dark blue. He removed the padlock and pushed the door open.

"Welcome." He gestured for her to go inside.

There was a musty smell, and something else…it smelled faintly like a butcher's shop. Jon banged around for a while and the sounds echoed harshly from the metal walls. A paraffin lamp came on.

In one end of the lock-up was a camping table and two chairs. At the other were blankets and cushions. All sorts of things – bottles and boxes and metal canisters –

were piled up against the walls.

"Have a seat." He indicated the floor.

Down at ground level the smell of butcher's shops was stronger. The skulking thought-creature showed itself in full light for a instant, and it was a creature she recognised. If she could just get the lock-up to stop swaying around, if she could stop feeling sick, if she could catch up with events, she would be able to remember what kind of creature it was.

Jon offered her more brandy but she refused it. He sat down, put his arm around her, put his hand on her cheek and turned her face to his. Then he tried to eat her.

Ordinary reality shattered into broken-mirror pieces. Elizabeth wasn't sure if it was a kiss – her first kiss – or not. There was something in her mouth, something both soft and hard, and alive. Her body was confused. She didn't know if it was nice or horrible. Jon smelled of smoke and drink, which wasn't nice at all. Weird explosions detonated within her, which suggested that it was nice. Her arms had wrapped themselves around his neck without her permission. She felt the softness of his skin and the silkiness of his hair, and the idea of his momentous beauty moved within her like a great wave – but the thing, that wet, too-soft, too-insistent tongue…it *was* horrible.

She tried to pull away, and instead found she was lying down on the blankets. Jon was all over her at once. One of her barely-there breasts was exposed, and that really couldn't be – that was so very, very wrong.

"No," she said, and when nothing changed, "No! No! Stop it! Leave me alone!"

"It's all right, Liz. It's fine. I won't get you into trouble. I'm not stupid."

"Jon – no!"

She struggled, but whatever she tried, it had no effect. He did bizarre, shattering things, and she wasn't strong enough to stop him. Now she couldn't keep up with events at all: the runaway train of her life was completely out of sight. She kept struggling. She'd heard of women sticking their fingers in men's eyes, but she couldn't make herself do that. Besides, he had hold of her wrists.

By the time there was a terrible pain and she realised it was really too late, she wished, fiercely, that she hadn't cared about hurting him, that she had fought harder. The pain got worse, and worse. She screamed. Screaming felt good. It felt right. The burning dog flashed into her mind and she screamed with everything she had. Then she did manage to push him away.

"Shut up! What the hell's wrong with you? You sound like a loony."

Jon was kneeling, fastening his belt. She grabbed at clothing, pulled it back on as quickly as he'd torn it off.

She backed away from him until she was pressed against the cold, ridged metal wall. At last, she had the thought-creature by the tail. She knew. She knew what she had really guessed, and hadn't allowed herself to believe.

"You did it, didn't you? You burnt William's hut?"

"Me and Darren. Yeah, we did. You'd best not say anything though – wouldn't be too good for you *at all* if you did."

The atmosphere of the lock-up jumped at her, threw itself over her like a vat of farmyard slurry. It had been revolting all the time but she had refused to see it. Jon was still kneeling. She looked down on him. A worse horror rose and she swallowed bile. She knew something else, something that she hadn't even begun to guess before.

"And the dogs. You and Darren. You killed the dogs."

Jon laughed. "Don't worry, darlin' – there won't be any more dogs. Dogs are only fun for a while."

Elizabeth lurched for the door and ran. She knew he wasn't following, but the horror stayed with her. It was in the imprint of his hands, in the pain between her legs, in the stink that he must have left all over her, a stink as strong as petrol poured over an animal. She ran, tripping and recovering and tripping.

She had heard the music here for the first time, and it had made her want to dance along this cliff. She hadn't danced, because people would have laughed and thought her strange. Now she didn't care. It was the rest of the world that was insane.

Tomorrow she would find William. She would find him, and she would dance with him, and dance, and dance.

Adnan Mahmutovic

Gusul

Emina, the not-quite-integrated Bosnian immigrant is working, but her work, the autistic boy Stig, is scuttling from gravestone to gravestone around Stockholm's Katarina Church, knocking over aluminum vases with yellow flowers, his long blond hair wet and glued to his face. He sings the latest Swedish hit that bombed at the Eurovision Song Contest, "I wanna be like a star like a hero, love will survive."

The ghosts of Sweden past that sit on the mossy and cobbled ground around the church seem very kind and cheerful to Emina. They do not look at her with derision. They do not seem to mind that she is looking straight through them as if they did not grace her with their presence. She is focused on the space between gravestones. The grave of Erik the smithy is well fenced, so that Ivar the baker and Irma the milkmaid do not enter his space like they used to do in the times when the city customs still meant more than the invisible barrier between the rich and the filthy rich.

Emina rests her eyes on the family grave of Gottfried the watchmaker and finishes her turkey sandwich. Her mother's old blue cardigan makes her look a decade older than her thirty-five. Her face is dry. She has forgotten again to apply the face butter from the Body Shop.

Stig loves the churchyard, where ghosts are so old they have few relatives to bother them with odorless flowers. Yet, there are always a few nostalgic descendants who honor the dead they found in some old record. Now there is a middle-aged couple, both with same crewcut and green rubber boots, working on a flower arrangement. They scowl at Stig as he does the Spider-Man impersonation in front of them.

"Stick härifrån, din lilla snorunge," the man hisses.

Emina stands up as if pricked in her heels, walks by

the green-fingered couple and catches Stig when he jumps between two granite gravestones. He laughs into her left ear and kisses her on the temple. She hates calming him down when he claims the open space as if there's no such thing as social borders. His autism usually keeps him silent and cornered in his classroom.

Emina puts Stig down. "Go and finish your McChicken. You have to be back home in half an hour." She keeps her back turned to the couple who keep muttering, "Låta pojken hoppa runt kyrkogår'n."

"Så oförskämt."

Stig scratches his ears under the soaked hair. "I want to see your mom, the superhero."

"The Superhero?"

"Yes, she's the Rogue."

"What's the Rogue?"

"Not what, who. She's the powerful X-Man who steals other mutants' powers. She has black and white hair. Like your mom."

Emina pulls him into her arms, removes his hair from his face, and presses her thin lips on his chin. "Tell you what, she is the Rogue, but you mustn't tell anyone. She's old now and has lost her powers."

"Cool. Is that why she doesn't speak?"

Emina folds up as if someone cut her sinews. A surge of memory makes her feel irresponsible, unfocused on the boy. Stig straddles her and peers into her pupils as if his eyes were a doctor's flash. He seems to be in charge, the grown up, even though carefree and happy.

She makes herself laugh, and says, "She doesn't speak because she's lost someone, a fellow hero."

"Cool."

"Yes. Very cool. If you talk to her, maybe she'll speak with you."

Stig cups his hands in front of his mouth and giggles. "Good goody good. When?"

"Maybe on Sunday. Your mom can drop you off after church."

"Don't like it. The preacher speaks strange."

Emina wants to ask him why he dislikes the priest, but then she remembers what his parents told her at the job interview. Stig's autism means he cannot understand general nouns, concepts, abstractions. He can't see how murder and jealousy are both sins, how Jesus can be both a man and a God. Emina once told him that maybe Jesus the man is the secret identity of Jesus the God, like Clark Kent and Superman. Stig said, "Cool."

Emina rests her head on the cobbles. Stig tears away to fetch the rest of his cold burger.

Emina walks into her apartment like she would step on a bus, as if to get somewhere. The damp walls smell of dogs even though it's been over a year since the old tenants moved out. She walks into the bathroom, washes her hands with peach soap, and smells her fingertips.

In the bedroom, her mother's body seems to have grown roots into her bed. The smell of urine does not prevent Emina from smiling. She kisses her mother on the cheek. "Mom, do you need to go to the toilet?"

The woman nods.

Emina lifts her up as if she's pulling a plant, gently, because she must place her back there once she has changed the soiled sheets.

The seventy-two-year-old woman coughs. Coughing, panting and snoring are the only sounds she communicates with. Emina can distinguish nine moods of her mother's mind from her snoring.

Emina changes the sheets, remembering how, four

years earlier, she stopped hanging white sheets in her backyard for fear they could be shot at like all the white flags during the Balkan war.

When the mother lies down again and starts snoring right away, Emina thinks her mother is just pretending to make her believe she feels better. But the snoring is real, loud, and, Emina thinks, *comforting*. She says, "Dear Mom, I never thought my greatest pleasure would be to hear you snore."

No reaction.

Emina laughs, takes up a picture of her father. He wears a white *ahmedija* on his head, typical for a Bosnian *imam*. She closes her eyes. The *ahmedija*, like a white flag, falls on the ground outside a small stone mosque with a blue tin roof. Some soil covers it as thousands of feet pass by pass by pass by. Grass grows out, and weed, the inedible things. There is more green now. Evergreen woods of Southern Sweden, and the meadows between them, and a gray highway spruced with colorful cars. Lots of red cars. Volvos and Saabs, and Volkswagens.

Emina opens her eyes and says without turning to her mother, "When I was a little girl you could never shut up."

She caresses the picture with the cleaning cloth. "Father was the *imam*, but you, you wrote his sermons. By Thursday night, you had his Friday *jummah* speech ready. You read it to us in a candle-lit kitchen, and we listened, and sometimes said, 'Do it again,' just to enjoy your voice."

She looks at the thin, eggplant-colored lips opening and closing in the rhythm of the twitches of the eyelids. She tries to remember the voice, but she can only recall images, as if she has been deaf all her life. She swallows spit three times.

"Remember the night our ferry arrived at Ystad,

where we spent our first week in that huge hangar with some two hundred chatting yelling farting refugees? The immigration officers questioned us: what kind of immigrant are you, how much money have you got on you, do you have relatives here, how long do you plan on staying?" She pauses. "You just kept silent."

The picture slips from her hand and falls on the floor. She picks it up, kisses the black and white, clean-shaven face, and puts it amid other pictures of herself as a baby, as a girl with braids, as a young woman with loads of emotions and equations in her mind, and as a genderless refugee outside a corroded bus holding the hand of a mute mother.

"Emina, my feet are cold," the mother says.

Emina keeps wiping the pictures. Then, as if the message was garbled and her brain took a while to decipher it, she stops, looking at the photo of her mother's wrinkle-less face as if it was that young woman who spoke to her. She turns around.

The mother says again, "Emina, my feet are cold."

Emina straddles the narrow bed, takes her mother by the calves, and presses the soles of her feet against her warm stomach. The tangled, purple veins seem to be glued onto the cellophane skin of the feet, rather than growing like weed underneath. Emina rubs the seventy-year-old skin. It creases, and the veins change patterns. She opens her mouth a few times to say something, but doesn't, for fear there is some limit to the number of words that can be said right there and then.

The mother smiles, and says, "I'd like some plum pie."

"Plum pie?"

She nods.

Emina stands up, tucks in the moist feet, and gives her mother some water. The woman swallows one clunk.

"I'll go and make you some pie." But she can't move. She kisses her mother on the lips and then gives her more water. She caresses her long grey hair, and the single lime-white lock. She thinks, *the Rogue, huh.*

In the kitchen, which is just outside the bedroom, Emina produces a bowl of dark plums, sugar, flour, oil, and a round earthenware dish as if everything was already right there ready at hand, just waiting for the wish to be uttered. Bosnian plum pie is a like a black sheep among all the different pies. Once cooked, it's more like plum jam with cream.

Emina pours oil into the dish, and says, "Mom, you know Stig. He said you looked like some super woman from his comic books, who absorbs other people's powers." She cracks open the plums and pulls out the stones with her teeth. She spits the stones into the kitchen sink, and lays plum-halves in circles in the dish. "I told him you're the one, but he must keep it hush hush."

She pinches some sugar and throws it on the plums. Then she does the same with flour, and finally pours cream until the plums swim in it.

Ten minutes in the hot oven, the plums are soft. She opens the oven and lets the dish simmer in the heat for five more minutes. Then she puts it on the windowsill and opens the window just a crack. The September wind wafts in. The mother's nose wiggles a little, but she can hardly breathe. She tries to say something, but her lips are clammy, saliva-white, the tip of her tongue pressing the back of her teeth. "L…l…la."

Emina rushes into the bedroom as if the nascent *shahada* was a bait. She fumbles as if the *shahada* is already pulling the old body over the thin and sharp *Sirat* bridge towards the open gates of *Jannet al-Adn.* She grabs her mother's face. "No Mom, not the *shahada*, not now, please, not the *shahada*."

The mother raises her voice and says twice, "La-ilaha-ilallah, Muhammedun Resulullah." The second testimony of faith pushes Emina backwards, like a hand. The mother's eyes close and her chest stops rising and falling.

Emina wipes the few tears and struggles not to cry. She sits on the bedside, her back turned to her mother. Then she slips under her quilt and covers herself up to her nose, like she did as a kid, before she started school and stopped fearing the shadows of the quince tree under the twin moons.

Later – she cannot tell how much later – Emina stands in the hall, watching the telephone as if waiting to hear it speak for her. She lifts up the receiver and pushes it under her black hair as under a hat. She punches the numbers with her knuckles.

"This is Fatima."

"Salaam-u-alaykum. May I speak with *imam* Atif?"

"Atif."

"Salaam-u-alaykum. This is Emina Begović."

"Alaykum-u-salaam."

"My mother has died."

"I'm sorry for your loss. She was a pious woman, she has moved on to a better world."

"I haven't cried."

"Good. The tears of the beloved ones burn the soul of the deceased."

Silence.

"Emina, have you called the medics, the morgue, anyone?"

"No."

He breathes out like a smoker. "All right. Then I'll

do it for you."

Emina presses the receiver harder against her ear. "Please let me wash her. Tuck her in one last time."

"Pull yourself together. This is most unusual. It's a ritual. We have women trained for that."

"Please, I need to do it. I must."

"Would you even know—"

"I've seen my parents *gusul* dozens of bodies. I could wash my mother with my eyes closed."

"Are you sure?"

"Yes."

"Do what you must. I'll arrange for a coffin."

"Coffin? Why coffin?"

"Emina, remember where you are. In Bosnia, we'd only sweep her into a white *ćefin*. The Swedish law prescribes a coffin."

"Thank you."

Emina watches the small daisy flowers on the wallpaper. Next she becomes conscious of her body, she is carrying the plum pie as if to an angry queen who has ordered it long time ago but never got it. She places it under her mother's nose and waits. The sweet smell fails to tease her back to life.

Another time lag. Another gap in the mind.

Now she is neatly folding her mother's quilt, a patchwork of all colors on earth. There is a smell. Unfamiliar. She inhales it, slowly, as if not to hurt the air.

She leans over the naked feet and unbuttons the pajamas, splays them open like a book she has been reading every day all her life, which she has dog-eared and where she has marked the important words, crucial phrases, stand-alone passages, favorite chapters.

She pulls out the pillow. The mother's mouth opens and the air remaining in her lungs blows out over Emina's right ear with the ease of the word "La," the negative, the negation before the affirmation.

Emina tears a white towel with her teeth. She dips each of the five pieces into a bowl of lukewarm water, squeezes out the water and dabs the body. The dark veins branch out from the ankles like the foot of an up-rooted tree.

Emina can still smell the plums.

She washes the soles first, washes off her own sweat that rubbed off when she warmed the feet. She moves the wet cloth up her mother's slender thighs up to the vagina. Next she cleans the scar from the Cesarean. She recoils as if she's seen it for the first time. She thinks, *I've forgotten they cut me out of you.*

She almost skips the breasts, which look uncannily young, and small, as if they've never fed a baby, or been kneaded by a man. She moves up to the chin, with three long hairs, which the mother never let her pull out.

Then she moves aside, over the shoulder, down to the twin scars from the vaccine. She caresses the indigo hand, strokes it and pulls off the ring. She presses the hand against the bed, but it moves up a little and then falls back onto the bed.

Emina washes the ears, and takes time whispering, "Eudubillahi mina shaytan irrajeem. Bismillahi-rrahmani-rrahim. Ja-Seen. Wa Al Qur'anil hakeem…"

When she tips her mother on the side to tighten a white sheet around her the way mothers wrap babies so their bodies will grow straight, she thinks she can hear her collarbone cracking. She places her mother's thin braids over the breasts and lays her head on the edge of the bed.

The phone rings.

Emina picks up the receiver.

Atif says, "Emina, I've notified the authorities. Someone will come to take her to the morgue."

"I'm done. Mother looks like she did on *hajj*, twenty years ago."

"Listen to me, this isn't Bosnia. We can't bury her today. I'll speed things up, but it'll take at least three days."

Emina hangs up.

She takes the plum pie and half a loaf of hard, whole-wheat bread, and goes out the front door. She sits down on the staircase. The buzzing bulbs color the plums yellow-green, like toxic waste. She digs out the soft heart of the loaf, puts it into her pockets, chops off pieces of the crust, and scoops up plums. She does not chew. She gulps and gulps until the food sinks down her throat. She takes another bite, and one more before swallowing the first.

Two men in yellow vests walk into the building with a stretcher. A man that looks like a clean-shaven albino bear, and with no expression on his face asks, "Where?"

Emina swallows and opens her mouth as if to say something, but she only points with her whole hand and goes on choking on the plums and the bread until she hears the ambulance drive off.

Stig jumps from gravestone to gravestone in the Muslim section of *Skogskyrkogården*. Most stones have a crescent and a star carved close to the top, a name or names underneath. A few even have a small white bird perched on the last letter of the surname. Emina stares at a group of graves so close to each other as if the people in them were relatives. But, Ahmed the Egyptian, Zuleyha the Pakistani, Osman the Albanian, Safiya the Malayan, and Ibrahim the Somali don't say much to each other. They speak to Emina, in their native tongues. A small-time town of Babel. Emina imagines they are gesticulating to help her understand their afterlife troubles. Her mother is still silent.

Stig shouts to Emina, “Look at this.” She lifts her eyes from the mound marked with her mother’s name. Stig jumps off Zülfikar the Turk’s marble gravestone, bends his legs and spreads his arms as if he is going to hug her. He presses his palms with his two middle fingers, to release the spider-web, and yells, “Pfzzzz, pfzzzz.” He falls flat on his stomach, and a second later he’s up again. He pulls up his Spidey-suit, and points at his skinny torso. “See, no injuries.”

Alex Barr

Homecoming

It was only the plants they had to leave. Everything else went into crates. Bernard screwed down the lids while Rosalind noted the contents in a jotter. Before they even thought of checking the time, a big blue and green van appeared. The transfer company, five minutes early. The crew made breath clouds through their scarves in the subzero cold. Lit by the bright Kansas sun the boxes with their shadows looked solid. In fifteen minutes everything they owned was loaded.

The furniture was staying to be collected. Voluntary repossession. Their furniture had always been on credit, successive waves of it. This was the last wave. Bernard wandered through the bright rooms saying goodbye to it: the combination bed head and shelves covered in soft vinyl, the bookcase with trim that looked like brass but was paper. He remembered the spring day they ordered it all, from Mr Green's on Hydraulic Avenue where even the parquet was painted green. He remembered the high they felt when they found that, even with the business faltering, they could still get credit. Those were they days.

Bernard's ex-partner Wayne arrived to drive them to the airport motel. It was cosy in the cab, the three of them wedged together, Wayne smelling of Dentyne. Rosalind looked behind, at the suitcases in the back of the pickup, out in the cold. She felt neat and clean, her feelings packaged.

Wayne pulled out onto Eighteenth and paused for a moment so they could look back. At the front room window were the big cut-out leaves of the philodendron she and Bernard got in a garage sale when they first arrived. On the sill were the sawtooth leaves of the aloe their daughter Lesley brought them from Arizona. Rosalind and Bernard caught one another's eyes. They both pulled faces and raised their eyebrows.

'It doesn't have that reproachful look,' said Rosalind, 'like it always did when we left to go on holiday.'

Bernard nodded. 'I know what you mean.'

Now it was just a container, a box they'd lived in, storm windows worn but neat ready for the next owner. The frost on the porch rail glinted. Beyond, the swing seat moved in the icy wind, brilliantly sunlit. Bernard remembered all those summers, Lesley with bunches, in dungarees stroking a guinea-pig, or riding on his back pulling his ears. Lesley and Rosalind crosslegged on a blanket, laughing, racing to eat popsicles before they melted.

'Okay, folks?' Wayne asked.

'Okay,' they said.

He drove away fast.

At the motel they dumped the suitcases onto ribbed concrete which someone had marked with a finger *PG '91*. They hugged in a circle.

'So long, old horse, old buddy,' said Wayne. 'So long, Roz, you fantastic lady. And if you get to Italy, hello to Lesley.' He paused and looked at their faces. 'Hell, I wish things had've worked out.'

'Recession is…recession,' said Bernard. He wanted to feel some pain, to prolong the moment, but there was just this dryness, and the biting cold. They released each other.

Rosalind said, 'We came with five hundred pounds. We're leaving with five thousand dollars. It's not so bad.'

Wayne smiled. 'Guess you about kept up with inflation.' They tried to fix his smile in their minds.

'Home,' Bernard told himself. 'Not abroad, home.'

The big black taxi moved quietly through grey light. It was like being under the sea, Rosalind thought. The bare plane trees left a disturbing amount of sky. They didn't arch over to form a vault like the trees in their street in Kansas. The taxi turned onto the road where Terry lived.

'I know this road,' Bernard told her, surprised. 'I used to come this way to school. There were no trees then.'

The taxi stopped. Rosalind peered out. So this was Manchester.

'I even remember this house,' he said.

He'd walked past it day after day. First in new cap and blazer. Later, hoping to avoid the searching eyes of prefects, smoking Woodbines to calm exam nerves. This roof had been here then, with its lozenge pattern of lighter coloured slates. As well as this gable with scalloped barge-boards. Waiting years and years for his brother to buy it. But houses didn't wait, did they? Houses didn't know there was a future.

Terry opened the door. 'Well.'

He was shiny-bald. Rosalind hardly recognised him. But of course, she hadn't seen him since he married Jill well before Gulf War I. Whereas Bernard had seen him a year before Gulf War II, at their father's funeral in Abergele. By that time he was thinning. He shook Bernard's hand crisply and briefly, a business handshake. When Rosalind hugged him hard he looked embarrassed.

'Come along in.'

But there was a great deal in the way, wooden gate, iron gate, porch door, front door, hall furniture, living-room door. Their suitcases came to rest looking forlorn, Bernard thought, after the bumps and scrapes.

'So', said Terry, with a round Mancunian 'o'. He looked at them briefly, then at the room, as if trying to guess how it seemed to them.

'So here we are,' said Bernard. 'How's Jill, Terry?'

'Off on holiday.'

Bernard and Rosalind sank into unfamiliar chairs while Terry made a pot of tea. A young woman in Lycra leggings with short blonde hair came in. An au pair, perhaps.

'Oh, hiya,' she said, and rummaged in a pile of magazines. Rosalind suddenly recognised her profile. It was their niece Angela. She waited for her to find what she was looking for, then hug them and ask, 'What was it like in the States?'

'Well, see you.' Angela went out with a mail order catalogue. It was Terry, when he brought the tea, who asked the question. Bernard and Rosalind looked at each another. Where could they start?

Rosalind began, 'Different from here, for sure. I've noticed several differences already.' She paused, about to begin the list, and was saying, 'One is—' when Terry cut in.

'These madmen. These militias. Sounds like you got out just in time.'

Rosalind looked puzzled. They didn't know any militia members. A fellow in Mulvane drove a Humvee, but he was a loner, unconnected.

'Of course,' Terry grinned, 'you were into uniforms, Bernard.'

'What?'

'In your business.'

'Not uniforms, Terry. Work wear. Contract hire of work wear.'

Terry smiled broadly. 'Do workers in the States really have their name on their overalls? On a little embroidered badge with *Dave* or *Sue*?'

'Of course.'

Terry's face turned pink with amusement. They realised he was laughing silently. He laughed for a long time. They joined in politely, briefly.

In return for two months' food and lodging, Bernard was to help Terry in his electrical repair business. That had been arranged by letter. 'Further ideas when you get here.' Bernard thought this referred to a possible partnership, but as days went by and they fell into a routine Terry seemed to feel no need for discussion. When he talked it was to complain about the council, the VAT, or customers with delusions about prices.

By the second week Bernard was agitated. The heavy wire screens on the windows made him feel caged. The radio channel Terry favoured played songs he'd known in his youth. It was as if for forty years nothing had happened. As if he'd never left Manchester.

'Terry,' he said suddenly halfway through a slack morning. 'This is your decision, okay? But if there's some way I can fit in permanently, into this organisation I mean, tell me.'

Terry didn't look up and nod and say, 'Sure, Bernard, I'll think about it.' He just scowled at the rusted terminals on a solenoid he was fixing. 'Shit,' he said.

After a moment Bernard added, 'If there's anything I can do.'

'You name it,' Terry said dully, still not looking up.

'So, the scenes of your youth,' said Rosalind.

He was showing her the playground in his old primary school. It was hard to believe so much had happened in that small hard space, feuds and alliances, fights and friendships, games of 'stag' and five-stones. Hard to believe that, apart from getting smaller, it hadn't changed. They leaned their elbows on the green railings that had once loomed above Bernard like the walls of Jericho.

They walked round to the chip shop where he first set eyes on his first girl-friend. The girl herself had married and taken a surname he didn't know. Amazing: it was still a chip shop with white cracked tiles and brown plastic vinegar-shakers. In a third of a century nothing had been lost—except a sense of anticipation.

Rosalind felt she couldn't breathe. So these urban crannies were Bernard and Terry's patrimony. She herself had been brought up on different farms all over the South, with aunts and uncles, while her parents built and sold—or tried to sell—pipe organs to fairgrounds. She'd spun round in sunlit fields of barley-stubble till she fell down. She loved the dizziness, the confusion of up and down, the way the earth fitted against her back as if she were the one supporting it.

'Show me the hills,' she said. 'A stone circle if there is one.'

She'd met and married Bernard in Southampton. Till now, all she'd seen of the North was Terry and Jill's wedding in Wilmslow. They hired a car, even though they thought it an extravagance, and set out for Arbor Low. They drove down the A6 through Stockport. In Hazel Grove they came to a standstill, then crawled at slower than walking pace. Bernard beat his hands on the wheel.

'Goddamn! What's all this traffic? What's happening today?'

'Maybe it's always this bad.'

'You could drive to the hills in half an hour. What's gone wrong?'

'Relax, Bernie, there's no hurry.'

But the tiny car oppressed him. The traffic was packed impossibly tight, the lanes were too narrow. The truck in his mirror was too close. Each time the traffic ahead moved on a yard or two, it roared impatiently and jerked forward. Bernard began to delay moving on, leaving a long gap ahead. The truck hooted. Bernard left even longer gaps. The truck pulled sharply into the inside lane, to aggrieved hooting from other traffic, and roared past.

'Did you see that?'

'Stay calm.'

He drove on, steeling himself to the ridiculous fits and starts, holding back the things he wanted to say. He looked for a King's X or an Uncle John's where they could pull in and have coffee. Where they could look across a booth at each other, where he could say, 'Who are these people, where are they all going? And why in cars? I thought in England people still walked or cycled.' Where he could say, 'I'm scared, Roz, what are we doing here? What am I doing with my life?' But there was nowhere like that here, only the odd small café straight onto the pavement, with no conceivable way of stopping outside. He was carried on in a slow tide of vehicles.

Out in the hills the road became dual carriageway. This was new. Bernard thought he recognised farms and hidden valleys he'd once seen at the mid-point of long walks, miles from a road. He slowed to look. It was hard to tell. He stopped. Traffic blared and swerved past him.

'Bastards!'

'I think that sign means don't stop.'

It was an X in bleached-out red on a blue disc.

'It means Mac Fisheries,' Bernard told her.

'What?'

'When I was a kid there was a Mac Fisheries in every high street. White X on a blue disc with four white fish.'

'There are no fish on that one, Bernie.'

'No, the seas have been trawled to death.'

Rosalind looked at him coldly. 'I want to go home.'

'Home?'

'You know what I mean. Home is wherever I'm staying.'

Bernard sat unable to move. She got out, went round, and opened the driver's door. Cars flashed and hooted. She prodded him and he moved across automatically, as he did if he was half asleep when she came to bed.

Rosalind found work, making phone calls for a bank to explain a new savings scheme. The call centre had a thick atmosphere of anxiety and a fast turnover of staff, but it would do for now. Bernard stopped trying to discuss the future with Terry. He forced himself to go through the local paper, passing *Brownies take to the stage* and *Off-licence knife attack* to reach Business Opportunities. There he read *This is what you've been looking for.* The advert was signed *Ken.*

Ken lived in a brick duplex—no, Bernard corrected himself, a brick semi. He was small and intense, with liquid eyes and a goatee beard. Every surface was piled with papers. The phone kept ringing. Business seemed to be good.

'So you've been in the States? Useful experience.'

Bernard couldn't pin down Ken's faint accent. Australia? Birmingham? He wondered what Wayne was doing right now. Maybe this very thing. The old partnership had compressed to the nugget *experience*, like a forest crushed into coal.

'Business is business, Bernard. Whether it's work clothes or these little critters.' He handed Bernard a lump of metal. 'They go on fuel lines and save fuel. You can read all the science in this leaflet, but let me tell you, they work. Figures prove it.'

Bernard hefted the thing and turned it over. It was stove-enamelled a nice daffodil yellow. He put it down and studied the papers. There were testimonials from well-known firms, saying how fast they'd recouped their capital investments. He could feel Ken's eyes on his face, trying to construe his thoughts.

'But people are so hard to convince,' Ken went on. 'Suspicious. That's the bugger of it. And I need good people.'

Bernard picked the thing up again. It was solid, for sure.

'I need time to think.'

'Of course you do, Bernard. You must feel unsettled, just back in the UK. Tell me, do Native Americans really hug trees when they feel unhappy, or is that an urban myth?'

Bernard stared. He thought of young Cherokees, shown round the firm on work experience. How dazed they'd looked, as if their souls were off visiting elsewhere. He thought of the sullen Navaho help in South-western diners.

'Never heard that, Ken.'

'Well Bernard, maybe *you* should try it.'

Bernard laughed. The laugh relaxed him. He drank the coffee Ken had made and suddenly felt fine. Maybe this unlikely product was okay. Ken seemed okay. It didn't matter about his Nowhere accent, that was just prejudice. Wherever he was from, he'd chosen Manchester. So it would be okay for Bernard and Rosalind to live here.

'So where would I hug a tree, Ken? Chorlton Park?'

Ken pulled a face. 'Nowhere here, Bernard. Haven't

you felt it?'

'Felt what?'

'That the energy is blocked.'

Ken looked at him intently, eyebrows raised, as if to say *Significant moment—trust being established.*

'So why do you live here?'

Bernard was aware that his voice was sharper and higher.

'Good place to do business. Fortunately I have a little retreat in Cornwall. I go when I can.' A long pause. 'Convinced yet?'

In the States Bernard would have said, 'No Ken, I'm not.' Now he just looked away and shrugged.

Rosalind said slowly, 'Perhaps it was a mistake.'

'What?'

'Coming here.'

Bernard said angrily across the dining table, 'How can you say that? You think we can just pack up and go somewhere else? Where? How do we decide where? Drive round the country like tourists? How long will our stash of money last at that rate?'

Rosalind looked outside. In front of the clouds a 747 strained upwards with a noise like an over-revved motor-bike. In the kitchen Terry, washing up, coughed. From Angela's room came a faint thump of music.

Bernard sighed. 'We should have known it would be like this. We should have psyched ourselves up for it.'

A pause.

'I wanted to see you in your old home,' Rosalind said. 'To catch some of that belonging second hand. It's what all my life I thought I'd missed. But maybe it isn't something real.'

He didn't know whether she meant it or was just being provocative, advertising herself in some way. He thought about the playground again, and suddenly longed for the certainties of childhood. The girls who were mysterious and unsullied. The boys you could be angry with and wrestle, then friendly with again. The games of sheriffs and outlaws you never doubted were worthwhile.

'What do you mean?' he asked.

'Maybe there's no such thing as belonging any more.'

'Why not?'

'Because…' She couldn't explain. Because of technology? Fashion? Pollution? Globalisation? No, there was something else underneath it all, something she couldn't get at. 'Because everything is up for grabs.'

'What does that mean, Roz? What the fuck does that mean?'

'Don't talk to me like that. It wasn't exactly what I meant.' She thought, *There's no exploring together any more, no groping in the dark and finding a friendly hand.*

Bernard said, 'Well if you can't say what you mean, shut up. And stop casting gloom. Over there you got away with casting gloom because people were so upbeat, but don't do it here, right?'

She looked through the window angrily. The sky was still ruled into lines with contrails. The sound of dishwashing had stopped, apart from a plate being moved carefully now and then.

He went on, 'And stop saying it was a mistake to come here. I do belong. So—'

'For God's sake get off my back!' Now it was too late, anger was in her head like rods. 'Stop saying, "stop saying". If you hadn't kept saying "stop saying" you might have heard my warnings, the business might not have failed.'

A terrible silence. Not a plate to be heard. Angela's

music repeated the same pleading phrase. Bernard picked up a mug to throw on the floor, then realised it wasn't his. And the floor was carpet, not ceramic tiles like they'd had in Kansas, so it wouldn't have smashed anyway.

He went to Angela's bedroom. The door was open, she was sitting on the bed reading *Hello!* magazine. He knocked and walked in but she didn't hear him. When she saw him she jumped up and backed away. Her eyes slid all round the room. Bernard turned off the music.

'Will you lend me your bike?'

'What? I don't know.'

'Just say yes or no, Angela.'

'I suppose.'

Which way? The Cathedral, perhaps, built on a rock outcrop, even though streets had risen around it and changed the topography. The day was damp and not cold, not like winter—or any other season. He cycled past Manchester City football ground. A huge new stand in some pale metal soaked up the pale grey of the sky.

The surrounding streets of terraced houses echoed with isolated shouts. Women with thin white legs hurried along with pushchairs, as if the street wasn't where they wanted to be. Young men laughed, clustered round cars, hands cupping cigarettes. Cars crawled by throbbing with music from open windows. Bernard had once walked down this street with his father, and an old woman had said, 'Here y'are love,' and given him a mint imperial.

He cycled on. Yes, it had changed—for the better, he decided. Roz was wrong—he still felt waves of anger against her—a place could change and you could still belong. This neighbourhood had been a backwater, now it was a miniature Bronx or South Central L.A. Richly diverse, and—

He was going to be killed. Then he wasn't. He was just half off his bike, his heart like ice, with the front of a car six inches away. It had shot out from a side road without warning and halted with a terrifying squeal.

He wrenched the bike sideways and came alongside the driver's door. His legs were trembling.

'Idiot! Jerk! Moron!'

A youngish man swore back at him in some strange rhythmical code of unrecognisable words. Bernard rode on. The exercise calmed him. But when he stopped at a red light it occurred to him that the man might not take all that lying down. And indeed two or three cars behind was the roar of a gunned engine.

The lights changed, he rode on slowly, apprehensively. Before he could look round he felt the slipstream as the car shot past a few inches from him. It squealed to a halt ahead, at an angle to the pavement. There was something appalling about that angle.

Bernard looked for an escape route. He saw a passage between backyards, paved with setts, littered with used nappies and plastic bags. He took it. Brick walls went by in a blur. The fear gave him a feeling of elation. *But this is my home,* he thought, *Manchester not L.A. This shouldn't happen.*

He shot across the next street, looking out for the car. No sign—but he could imagine it about to squeal round the corner, right down on its offside springs. He pedalled into the passage opposite, slowing, his legs tiring.

It was like the way he once walked to school. As a small child he thought Manchester was formed of passages, like Venice with its canals, the air heavy and thick with smells from breweries and old men's pipes. Number One Passage, Number Two Passage, all the way up (he thought then) to Number One Million Passage. They were the heart of everything he'd belonged to. What number was this one? He didn't dare slow to look. What number would he die in?

He came out onto another street, quiet, without traffic, and turned left. Then right onto Moss Lane East. A sign said Universities. So there were two now. And a new cycle route along the edge of Whitworth Park. He took it. He was safe.

Passing Oxford Road station he decided to take a train. He got on the one that was waiting, not bothering to see where it went. He stayed in the parcel van with the bike, peering out to see how much he remembered, but the scenery made no impression on his mind. His thoughts went in angry circles—the argument with Rosalind, the traffic jam in Hazel Grove, the failed business, the unknown future, Terry's blankness, the man who'd nearly killed him. When the conductor came he asked for the next station and got off.

It was Bramhall. It came back to him, as he passed through the village, how he used to cycle here in his youth, with friends. If he kept his gaze high, on the familiar roofscape, and ignored the brash new signs, he could imagine it unchanged. He took the road uphill towards Woodford, his thigh muscles tingling. The air smelt fresh, the wind was cold and bracing. The houses were neat behind well-kept hedges. It was all soft and green and muted, not hard and red and echoing like Manchester. *I could live here,* he thought. *To hell with Roz, she can take it or leave it.* He went over things she'd done, mistakes, omissions, to stoke his anger.

Where the road levelled out there were fields on his left. It was still almost countryside. Beyond the fence to his right, JCBs at work. A new housing estate, perhaps. That was a pity, he remembered that field full of barley. Or was it wheat? Roz would know—but damn her, it didn't matter. He turned right past cottages, nurseries, market gardens. Memories came back. He and John Rose had parked their bikes by an oak and wandered through these fields, pulling at grasses, talking about girls they admired, about the future, what they were going to do with their lives. Perhaps the oak was still there—after all, they lived a thousand years.

It was.

It hung—seemed to hang—on the edge of an abyss. An enormous channel, a new kind of space.

The country lane was suspended over nothing. Aliens had loaded acres of greenhouse, wood, hedge, fence, and grass into a spaceship, and beamed in concrete to hold what was left together. Giant aliens, who lived at a different scale.

The new road marched east and west. Now Bernard saw that what he'd seen from the other lane wasn't housing. It was this road about to break through. Every path across fields had been severed like a nerve.

He wheeled the bike through the back gate of Terry's garden. It was a rectangle of coarse grass with one cherry tree and one mallow. As he shut the shed door on the bike Rosalind came down the five steps from the house and barred his way. Terry and Angela looked down from the kitchen window.

'Jill's gone,' she said. 'Left for good.'

'Good God. Has Terry just told you?'

'No way. But he can't tell me where the atlas is, or the ironing board, or the Joni Mitchell albums. You don't take all that on holiday.'

'Damn!'

'Why couldn't he tell us? Why?'

Rosalind scrutinised his face with a hurt expression. Bernard felt scoured clean by her gaze. He had no secrets from her, or at least, only the one, the big one he'd have to tell her now. Because holding back had made it seem not real. Like not going to the doctor, because once you went you admitted you were sick.

She looked into Bernard's eyes. They were alike, the two brothers, but one hadn't moved, hadn't changed from childhood, whereas this one, the one she'd helped to mould, for him there was hope.

He took her hands, steadying her as if to announce a death.

'Listen.'

'Go on.'

He took deep breaths. 'It's just…oh Jeez. This is awful.'

'Bernard, come on.'

He cried out, 'It's a mistake. A terrible mistake, coming here. Oh God. I'm paralysed. I can't think. I can't imagine a new business. All I can think is places. Places, places, places. We don't belong anywhere, not anywhere on this earth.'

Rosalind's eyes were wet. She kept her hands joined to his and pushed at him, wrestling him like an enemy. Terry and Angela continued watching as if it were a TV drama.

'I hate you,' she said. 'I hate you.' She twisted his wrists trying to hurt him. 'For keeping everything hidden and putting me through hell before you crack. Then you're like a weed.'

'This is awful,' Bernard said. There it was again, the scrunching between his heart and stomach. Wrong, it had all gone wrong. 'And the boxes haven't even come yet.'

'Well that's good.'

He stared at her. What did she mean? That now she'd go off like Jill, maybe live in Italy with Lesley? And he'd say, like Terry, 'Roz is on holiday.'

'You think it's good.'

'We aren't slaves to that stuff. To a cause. Or even to one another.' She was still trying to break his wrists and fingers. 'Don't call it a mistake. Just say we trialled and errored.'

He laughed. Rosalind laughed. In the steamed-up kitchen Terry and Angela rubbed at the glass.

She said, 'Tried and erred. Wrong turning. Back to the junction, try again.'

'Italy?' he murmured.

Rosalind shook her head. 'Lesley would feel dumped on.'

'We don't belong anywhere, Roz.'

'We belong together.'

Her words tumbled around in Bernard's mind, not making sense. *I hate you. We belong together.* Distracted, he forgot to push. She drove him back until he was against the brick garden wall. She was gritting her teeth, and beyond her wild hair the sky was a mass of contrails broadening into scarves of cloud. He thought, *I want clouds made by God, not man,* and angrily shoved her backwards. In the centre of the sour-looking grass she matched his strength again. Stalemate.

By now they were both in tears.

'All—those—partnerships,' she gasped. Then after a deep breath, 'Wayne—failed. Terry—failed. Look at him.'

She sidestepped, turning them until Bernard saw the kitchen window framing Terry's blank white cipher of a face.

'Then Ken—no go,' she muttered.

'I didn't quite trust him.'

'You don't trust *me*. *I'm* your partner. *I* am.'

Tears were streaming down her cheeks. The sad garden, the dark red bulk of the house, the dishonoured sky, froze like a painted backdrop, old and rumpled. Rosalind's face was new, as if he'd never seen it before. The play of feeling around her mouth and eyebrows. The way her eyes burned into him.

They heaved and heaved, and each felt the other's power, and the grip of the other's feet on the earth.

Mary O'Shea

Out of Season

HE COMPLAINED ABOUT NOTHING, knowing the trouble she'd gone to. No one could be blamed for the hurricane blowing through the town or that their room didn't have a view of the sea or that this was going to be his last holiday. Salthill would never be St. Tropez, April would never be August and the pain behind the scar on his stomach would never go away.

'I thought,' Rita said, as soon as she recovered from the shock of seeing the room, 'that we'd have a sea view. I said on the phone -'

'You said on the phone you wanted single beds,' the woman declared. 'The rooms at the back of the house are all doubles. *They're* the ones with the view. The singles are at the front.'

Rita looked at the narrow beds and he thought for a moment she was going to cry. But she nodded and said: 'All right. We'll take it.'

Once they were alone he lay down. He closed his eyes against the cracked mirror over the wash-hand basin, the brown wave of a watermark sprawled across the ceiling, against Rita, at the foot of the bed, her hands clasped below her breasts.

'We should find somewhere nice, Charlie,' she said. 'It's not the time to be saving money. We can't stay here.'

'It's not the Ritz,' he conceded, unwilling to move. 'But it'll do. All seaside guesthouses are the same. There's no point in looking for better.'

'I should have asked more questions.'

'It's no one's fault. What I *would* like,' he said, with constrained gentleness, 'is to sleep for a while. Will you take my shoes off for me?'

She removed his shoes and stood with them in her

hands, staring at them. To go on holiday at a time like this, he realised now, was a very bad idea. She moved to the window and stayed there, looking out on the street, while sleep bore down on him.

When he woke up, she had a smile on. 'Feeling any better?'

He closed his eyes.

'Are you in form for a walk, Charlie, or would you like us to go and get something to eat?'

'I'll tell you when I'm awake.'

'You're not going back to sleep?'

'I'm still asleep.'

'You won't have a good night if you stay there any longer.'

He did not stir. Resting had not relieved the fatigue induced by driving across from Tipperary. It would be nice to be left alone for a while, then he could relax and maybe have a proper sleep. Rita's hovering made him tense. It wasn't reassuring to know you were being watched even while you slept, your breathing studied, your hours counted.

'I'm not hungry,' he said. 'Why don't you go off and get yourself something? When you come back we might go for a stroll. I can get a sandwich then, if I feel like it.'

'But you had no lunch. And you're not supposed to skip meals.' Her voice creaked with the unwholesome cargo of the past three months. As if food was the important thing. 'Besides, I can't leave you on your own like that.'

A remark made by the doctor as they were discussing the prognosis floated back to him: 'It can be easier to accept the prospect of our own death than the death of someone close.' At the time Charlie didn't think there could be anything worse than staring your own death in the face.

He took a deep breath and swung his legs over the side of the bed, asked for his shoes to be put on, smoothed his hair in front of the cracked mirror and put on his overcoat. Tomorrow she might be less brittle. There would be time enough to break away for an hour or two.

The wind on the promenade plucked at their coats, grabbing the edges and tugging them back. He felt stiff and weak, no match at all for the elements. The sky was the colour of gunmetal, the sea beneath its silver lid an angry winter green. They walked, arms linked, silent in contemplation of nature's cruelty. Last weekend had been so warm they had been able to sit out in the garden. They had thought how nice it would be to have a few days by the sea while he was still well enough. Now that they'd made the effort and come all this way, the seasons were reversed again, making a mockery of their optimism.

'A rough sea always makes me think of that May hymn,' Rita said. 'You know the one: *Thrown on life's surge we claim thy care*?'

'Star of the Sea? No, Hail Queen of Heaven. *Save us from peril and from woe.* You never hear words like peril and woe anymore.'

'No,' she sighed. 'There's such comfort in religion. It's a shame so many people have turned away.'

He knew it was good that she would take consolation there when he was gone. Yet it made him sad to think of her at early morning Mass, among a motley scattering of worshipers spread out in the shabby pews like survivors of some disaster too terrible to name, the responses carried over the vaulted emptiness by thin, cracked voices. Satan with his wickedness and snares had never been so free to roam the world. *May God restrain him, we humbly pray.* The balance sheet of clerical child abuse had amounted to a lot of damage. It was hard to believe all those accounts could be true. The subject had arisen in conversation during a recent family celebration for Rita's birthday. That was what he said: they can't all be true.

'Do you think someone's making it up, Dad?' Angela asked. 'Who, though? Buddhists? Hindus? The League of Atheists?'

'People exaggerate,' he said. 'And when there's compensation being handed out people will make things up.'

'My money is on Agnostics Anonymous,' Brian threw in. 'They're very active underground.'

'That's enough now,' Rita said, and it slid away.

Angela and Brian were, as far as he knew, earnest and good-living. They'd had their babies baptised but were not church-goers, and he doubted that prayer had any part in their busy lives. He did not know what he himself would have done without his faith. All he was grateful for was that his parents were not around to witness the demolition of every single thing they believed in.

'Is that a spot of rain?' Rita said. 'Maybe we should turn back.'

The wind, once it was behind them, was magnanimous, assisting them in their return.

The blow, minutes later, also came from behind. Hard and sudden, it landed on his back. He turned to see an orange beach ball bounce back onto the path. A boy of five or six, wearing a baseball cap, rushed to retrieve it and ran away. They stood outraged. A woman shouted 'Sorry!'

'You should have more control over your child!' The words quivered at the top of Rita's voice and were lost on the wind.

'You'd know by the get-up of her,' Rita said. 'Jeans and high heels, practically naked on top. When her children grow up to be delinquents she'll blame it on the state. That's the way they are nowadays: no respect for anyone.'

They'd had three: Brian, Angela and Fergus. There had been a miscarriage that Rita counted as a fourth but Charlie did not. Brian had fallen in for the shop. It was not too long before sweets and condoms joined the stock of hardware that had been for sale there since his mother's time. It was shocking but Brian insisted that survival depended on such concessions to public demand. Charlie and Rita had struggled on for as long as they could but in the end it was obvious that a choice would have to be made: learn to use a computer or hand the business over. They agreed that they were too old for that kind of learning. That was the start and the end of it. They gave up the shop, moved to a bungalow on the outskirts of town and turned a blind eye to all the things that followed in the wake of automation. They had acquired mastery of mobile phones but everything else remained a mystery to them. Now there was a profusion of things from which they were forever excluded: ipods, Facebook, YouTube, Skype, wii, podcasts. They were annoyed to notice that even quite serious programmes on the BBC ended with an invitation to follow on Twitter. *Twitter*?

Angela was bright. She had gone to university and qualified as a teacher. She lived in Kilkenny town with her husband and two children. And Fergus... The mere thought of him inflicted pain sharper than any scalpel. Rita always said they shouldn't blame themselves, they had done their best. But he knew she blamed herself anyway and he felt the weight of all the things he hadn't done that he might have done. He was haunted by the suspicion that something trivial would have made the difference. If he'd bought a piano when the boy was asking to learn. If he'd helped him take care of the hamsters instead of forcing him to get rid of them. If he had sat down and talked to him instead of cuffing him in the ear the time he started going wrong. If…if…if…

The thing was, as he mentioned to a Mission priest some years ago, he felt he hadn't done his best as a father. People rarely give their best, the priest told him, in anything sustained, like a relationship. 'Don't be hard on yourself,' he said. 'We're muddling through. We're all just muddling through.'

The relief he had drawn from this philosophy did not last. The priest was young. What did he know? And coming from England his standards wouldn't be quite the same. Charlie had allowed his guilt be assuaged by a false tongue. What good was it to know that nobody did their best? Everyone got the chance, what they did with it was their own business.

They had their evening meal back at the guesthouse. It consisted of fried steak and chips, covered in grease and looking as if they had been a long time cooked. They made no fuss: when you were past a certain age it didn't do to be complaining. They scraped some of the fat off and put the burnt chips to one side, each of them, like refugees, longing for home.

Without the crack, the mirror over the sink might just have been adequate for shaving or applying make-up. Rita applied hers knowing it would be patchy. The grey light of another sunless day mixed badly with the yellow fluorescent tube above. The crack distorted her face. Moving in a bit, she could just make out a smudge of Caribbean Glow beneath her right nostril. She'd been lucky to see that. She wiped it away and pressed on the powder.

This routine had become unexpectedly important since they'd got Charlie's diagnosis. At first she had been surprised at the changes in her face. The line of her mouth was thinner, the creases around it deeper, and her eyes had developed the perplexed look of a person waking up in strange surroundings. As soon as she was aware that this was the face Charlie would see, she invested in some new foundation and lipstick in shades she had not worn before. She also bought eye-shadow without realising that her eyelids were too far gone. The memory of what it cost was accompanied by a disproportionate bitterness.

She'd got into the habit of wearing her glasses more and smiling a lot because she knew it was only the mouth or the eyes that give you away. People said she looked wonderful, and they smiled back.

Charlie was waiting for her to finish so that he could wash and shave. Nothing annoyed him more than this new ritual. It was a strange time for her to start paying attention to her appearance, and she seemed so pleased when people complimented her. It was harmless enough, he presumed, only it made him feel more keenly his isolation.

His reflection was another reminder, a constant one these days. He had taken to lingering over the lathering process, concealing the expression of the mouth, filling the hollows with foam, making believe that the blade would plough its smooth path and restore it to the way it was before. But the blade was unable to alter the gauntness of the face that had lately come to be his and that he didn't want to own.

This morning it was even less familiar after the

strain of a sleepless night. Rita, having finished her titivation, turned to fold away their nightwear and pull up the bedclothes. He envied her routines. He envied the depth of sleep that kept her safe in the hours of darkness. It had kept her safe last night while he lay in torment.

It was after midnight when he heard the first sounds from the room behind. He noted the time on the watch Angela had given him for his birthday. First he heard the door close, a second later the bedsprings groaned. He imagined an unknown finger, the woman's probably, running down the same list of guesthouses Rita had scanned, dialling the same number with an entirely different purpose.

He imagined a room with a double bed and a view of the sea. There was no sound of drapes being drawn so the window would be an inky rectangle in the middle of a cheaply-papered wall, a large, floral pattern like theirs no doubt, framed by shabby curtains. The carpet might be stained, the mirror cracked, the ceiling discoloured, but they wouldn't notice any of that. Nor would they know that the wall separating them from him was a cardboard-thin partition.

He lay still, listening to the sounds, allowing the scene to arrange itself. The bed creaked and gave an occasional slap against the wall. Murmuring rose and swelled and fell. Crescendo, diminuendo, crescendo again, diminuendo.

It was a while before he noticed perspiration enveloping him like a sheet of wet muslin. It seemed a lifetime since he had felt such urgent need. Rita's deep, rhythmical breathing ebbed and flowed in the brief silences. He regretted the space between his bed and hers, occupied by a sturdy locker. Returning home after the operation he'd been so full of the feeling of his own destructibility that he'd suggested separate beds. Obligingly, she made up the twin beds in the guest room and they'd moved in there. He hadn't had the heart to tell her that what he really wanted was a room to himself. When booking the holiday she asked for single beds without consulting him.

He missed her warmth and her softness, her need for him. He knew he should be grateful for his memories of loving. Instead they filled him with a sense of loss, a yearning so raw it bordered on distraction. He could see it now: all unions, even that most tender, were transitory moments, bridges made of silk, appearing to span an impossible abyss. It was only when dawn was breaking around the edges of the blue curtains that he was permitted to take refuge from consciousness until the sound of Rita splashing water in the sink summoned him back.

She appeared easier in herself this morning. It would be possible to get away alone but he no longer wanted to. What he wanted was to walk the promenade beside her, feel her arm through his, listen to her voice. He wanted her to remind him of things he had forgotten.

A steady drizzle kept them indoors until after lunch. They sat in the small sitting-room reading the daily papers down to the last detail in the classifieds, neither of them willing to disappoint the other by suggesting an early return home, both wishing the weather would clear up enough to allow them get a breath of fresh air. At last, around two o'clock, they were able to venture out.

They took the same direction up along the prom as the previous day. A couple of elderly nuns smiled at them. A jogger in a blue tracksuit beat a determined path past them. The woman with the jeans and high heels was down on the beach playing ball with the child. She looked up as they came into line but they looked away.

'Wouldn't you think he'd be at school?' Rita said.

'At least the bite is gone off the wind,' Charlie said.

'If only the sun would shine.'

'There's a break, over there, on the far side.'

They stood and looked across the water to where the sun painted a yellow pool on the stony landscape.

'Lisdoonvarna's behind those hills,' Charlie said.

'Lisdoonvarna? It couldn't be!'

'You never cease to amaze me. You know where every blessed thing in the house is but you have no idea where you are once you get a mile outside Templemore.'

'I was no good at geography.'

The irritation had shown in his voice. He couldn't help it. It had nothing to do with geography or her hopeless sense of direction.

THE FIRST TIME HE SAW HER she was sitting on a chair outside the taproom, face tilted to the sun, waiting for her aunt. It was her second day and already it was a lot less entertaining than she'd been led to believe. He was in Lisdoon that summer because he had drawn the winning ticket in a raffle in aid of the church rebuilding fund and he had nothing better to do. Rita had assumed her sister's annual duty in accompanying their Auntie Ivy to take the waters. Neither of them had been there before. Nor did they ever return.

They fell easily into conversation. Within half an hour he knew that she was about to get engaged to a bank official by the name of Benedict Hogan. Within the same half hour she knew that his mother had recently died, that the hardware shop he had inherited from her was up for sale and as soon as it was off his hands he was going back to America where he had already spent two and a half years working in a button factory outside New York managed by his brother. Of all the places on earth, he told her, America was undoubtedly the place to be. 'So, you're a man of the world,' she said. He laughed and told her that Templemore and New York were the only places he really knew. He'd never been to Dublin or Cork, and the sum of his knowledge of Ireland was the journey to and from Shannon Airport.

The absolute nature of their plans put them at ease with one another. They met every morning outside the taproom and in the afternoons, while Ivy was taking her nap, they went off on Charlie's motorbike to the coast. By the end of the week, Charlie was no longer so sure about returning to America and Rita had lost a good deal of her enthusiasm for marrying Benedict Hogan. Still, no declarations were made and, although addresses were exchanged, there was no arrangement to meet again. He assumed, as he waved her and Auntie Ivy away on the Saturday morning train, that the original plans would stand.

That was before he spent his first full day without her. He lunched at the hotel and as he ate he felt her withdrawing from him on her journey home, leaving him in an expanding vacuum. He noticed, as if for the first time, the stiff walk of the old people, the unsteady hands that conveyed food from plate to mouth, the eyes which had the appearance of seeing incalculable distances. He noticed young people laughing, holding hands.

In the afternoon, he took the road north-west, travelling faster than usual, aware of the emptiness of the pillion, disturbing the dust on the summer roads as he sped along. The beach at Fanore was scattered with browning bodies. She had sat there beside him several afternoons and he could remember no crowds around them. All he saw was her, golden from head to toe. He went on to the Black Head where it was quieter. Then he stood on the south shore looking north, just as now he was standing on the north shore looking south.

He came back by the coast road and Ballyvaughan after sitting for hours on a rock, remaking his plans to include her. The stone hills were violet in the evening sun. He still remembered thinking how strange it was the way love changed everything.

'Let's keep moving,' Rita said. 'We'll catch our death hanging around.'

He had to steady himself against pulling away from her.

She didn't need to look at him to know he'd slipped back into himself. It was a habit he'd acquired in the early stage of his illness: going inside himself and shutting her out. One minute he'd be chatting, the next he'd be a continent away. She understood it was nothing personal, just his way of dealing with things, but it would have been easier for her if he could have shared with her what was going on in his head.

She had followed his gaze to the rocks across the Bay. This was a day that would be important to her later…as all the days would. She hoped she'd be able to recall the details. The pool of sunlight had vanished from the rocks. The sky was slate; the sea had the grey-blue colour of tempered steel, flecked with white. The beach was deserted, the park beside the leisure centre empty. A group of youths restlessly revving their motorbikes were shouting obscenities at one another. She would need to recall it as it was, this sombre, late-April afternoon, the wind coming in off the Atlantic and his arm holding hers against his side.

They walked on under a darkening sky. When the rain began they took refuge in the nearest hotel. They ordered tea and drank it while the sky discharged its burden in great sheets of water over the streets and the Bay, along the beach and down on the roof of the hotel annex.

The following morning he went out alone. Rita had the beginnings of a cold and was finally persuaded that it would be prudent to take an extra hour in bed. The sun was shining on this new day and a man was painting the wooden benches on the prom a curious shade of pink in preparation for the summer season. Charlie paused to watch him, thinking that people would be sitting there when he was dead.

He wasn't looking forward to being pure spirit. It seemed a cold alternative to life. He had enjoyed sunshine, laughter, love. If eternal bliss was all it was cracked up to be there would be no room for earthly pleasures. So little was known about death, it was easier for him to believe that he would be compensated for his losses in ways he couldn't comprehend.

The man painting the bench straightened.

'Wet paint,' he explained. 'It won't be dry enough to sit on till the evening. And that's only if the rain holds off.'

'It's all right,' Charlie said, momentarily amused that he was being regarded as a danger to himself. 'I wasn't thinking of sitting on it.'

The room with the double bed had not been used last night. Even so, he had been slow to fall asleep and when he did, he woke up several times. Since the operation he couldn't sleep properly at night any more. It was as though his body was arming itself with exhaustion for the endless repose of eternity.

The illness had split his life into two states as distinct from one another as if they belonged to different people: the perilous present, swinging him on its pendulum towards the moment of annihilation; the past, distant and unchangeable as the landscape of County Clare, friendlier this morning in the sunshine. Looking back over time, he could see clearly the route he had taken, all the major turning points precisely marked. Some of his choices were more a matter of chance than of planning. He had bent with the breeze when he might just as easily have resisted it.

What if he had not returned to Ireland when his mother fell ill? What if he'd gone back to America instead of settling down in the place of his birth and marrying Rita? Would it have made a difference in the end? Would he be standing now on a patch of sand somewhere beside Long Island Sound, looking across the same ocean from the other side with the same scar on his belly, a different set of regrets and wondering what if...?

Westward, between two promontories, the Atlantic was crystal-blue today, the horizon a pencil-fine, navy-blue line. He went down the steps onto the beach and began to walk in the direction of the gap until he was out of breath. With an ache in the backs of his legs he sat down on a rock and rested his head in his hands. Apart from Rita's trips to the shops he hadn't had much chance to be alone since he got sick. In those brief spaces he couldn't help stirring the dense, dangerous brew of the past and tossing in for good measure his fears of what the future might hold. The house seemed too small, too solid, more a place of incarceration, where traces of him would remain long after he was gone. There would be traces of illness and defeat, of wasting, dependency and pain.

This vast amphitheatre of sky and stone, sand and water would keep no record of him. With the sun warming his face and hands, the lap and suck of the sea like a heartbeat in his ears, the gulls wheeling and squawking, sea-smells redolent of special days, the thought came to him that, since death was inevitable, it had to be all right to die. If he could let go, simply accept, how much freer he would be. It was the prospect of leaving Rita that complicated it. That – more than anything – got in the way of acceptance.

She had always been the strong one but forty-nine years of marriage was not much of a training ground for solitary old age. She had her friends, of course, the hours she volunteered at the community centre, occasional weekends spent minding her grandchildren, her Bridge nights. At the Bridge club there were widowers, most of them leaning towards decrepitude, all of them lonely. He knew her generous heart: the thought of anyone taking advantage of her shot a hook into the pain in his stomach and dragged it up along his gullet into his throat. He'd already warned Brian about Fergus. 'I don't want him coming around making trouble for your mother,' he'd said. 'Promise me you won't let that happen.' He had made adequate provision for her but it wouldn't last long if she decided to turn herself into Mother Teresa.

Rita...

He wondered if when the moment came they would recognise it for what it was. Would it be clear, unequivocal, like a ship pulling out of port with him on deck, waving; her on the quayside, waving? He would, he realised with a flash of disappointment in himself, prefer to avoid that. He had a fear of goodbyes. All his life he had lacked the talent for easy leave-taking. And yet, it was important, this last one. It would be important to do it right.

When he raised his head he was aware of a movement out of the corner of his eye. Just when he ought to have been securely alone, the woman and boy rounded a rocky outcrop no more than a few yards away. He read on the woman's face, a dried-out, tired face, the same mixture of fear and surprise he was feeling at that moment. But his attention stuck on the boy's head: it shone pink and bald in the morning sun.

Charlie nodded as they passed.

'Not a bad day,' he said, clearing his throat of what seemed like a wall of phlegm.

'No,' she agreed. 'At least the sun is out.' Her voice was gentle but the accent rough.

He followed them with his eyes as they walked on. Nearing the town end of the beach, the mother put a baseball cap on the boy's head.

Rita was waiting for him in the bedroom, her face made-up, her lips a fatal shade of raspberry. He put his arms tightly around her.

'What's the matter?' he said, feeling her stiffen.

She drew back to look at him, her face creased with anxiety.

'You have to be careful.'

'Of you?'

'Of yourself, Charlie.'

'I'm sick of being careful.'

'Are you all right?'

'You know how I am.'

She relaxed against him, warm and still, her head tucked into the crook of his neck, her arms lightly around him.

'I've missed you,' he said.

'I've missed you, Charlie.'

The street outside flowed with the sounds of voices and traffic. Downstairs a door slammed. In the room the plumbing gurgled.

'Rita, I was wondering…'

'Hmm?'

'What would you think about us asking to move to a room with…a sea view?'

'A sea view?' She tilted her head and smiled at him: young again, giddy again. 'Oh, I'd like that too.'

A. J. Ashworth

Overnight Miracles

We are in the blackest part of night now.

There's no light from the broken streetlamps outside. None from the alarm clock sitting blank-faced from the power cut. I can feel him in the bed beside me but can't see him. He's just a mass, not moving. Pressing down on the mattress and distorting its shape in the same way a black hole deforms space-time. I could roll towards him and be lost, gone forever. But instead I clutch the sheets and hold still; trying not to breathe because breathing too loud or too fast might change things – create some shift in the fragile balance of the here and now, and all will be broken again.

I was the one who started this.

I bought two red candles from a shop near the river: clutched the cool tubes over my heart as I ran home. In the bedroom I unwrapped the clinging plastic from their pristine bodies; placed them opposite each other on the dressing table. Trying not to see my reflection in the mirror as I did this: the shadows of dark crescents beneath my eyes; the weak glint of wedding band.

One by one, I placed the other things between them; the way the woman on the phone had told me to.

The specifics don't matter, she'd said, her voice slow and hoarse, as if her body was drying out with each breath. *It's all symbolic.* There was the sizzle of burning tobacco as she sucked on a cigarette. *It's all about feeling, about desire. You have to absolutely want it.* Another sizzle. *And, more than that, it's about belief.*

There was a man's voice there, low, distant. It buzzed and stopped: a blinking striplight of sound.

She cleared her throat. *You've got to believe,* she said. And then she hung up.

·

The woman told me to get things: something dead, something alive, something of the ground, something of his.

I cried and fretted about what to get, stared at the cracks in the ceiling until my eyes hurt. And then I slept. In the dream that followed he watched me with eyes the colour of opals then looked up as a white bird flew over his head. When he dropped his eyes again and opened his mouth, there was a fly, a maggot and a mound of soil on his tongue. And when he closed and opened his mouth again they were gone.

When I woke I knew. I collected a crisped fly from the kitchen windowsill. Maggots from the fishing tackle shop. I scooped up earth from the garden. And the broken glasses from his desk.

The woman told me to wait, until the moon was full – mid-way through its cycle.

'Like him?' I asked. 'Mid-way between one place and the next?'

Something like that, she said and coughed until her parched throat almost crumbled into dust.

I counted the days to full moon; crossed them out on the calendar.

I wrote down the sounds the woman had given me – not words, just sounds – and practised them as if they were from God itself. At times my jaw ached from the shapes my mouth made. The long vowels, the 'ooh's, the 'o's – making their invisible smoke rings to another realm. Signalling him home.

Then, when the moon was white and whole, I lit the candles: my retinas aching at the sudden flare. I stuck my finger into the bowl of soil and made a hollow. Buried the dead fly and the maggot, covered them over and put his glasses on top. I made the sounds until the room started to vibrate. Until the bowl and the candles and the mirror all rippled, as if something had dipped a finger into the pool of this reality and was testing the waters.

Just when it got so strong that I was vibrating in my seat, the maggot broke through the soil, throwing its head blindly, wildly, beneath a triangle of broken lens.

Then the movement stopped. The ritual was over.

When I went to bed my heart was shaking, but nothing happened. The elastic hours made minutes mimic hours and hours, days.

That was last night. I didn't sleep. And all day today, in the grey daylight – nothing.

I stopped myself from phoning the woman, to ask what had gone wrong. I told myself to give it more time; that it was stupid to expect an overnight miracle. So I waited. Washed windows and scrubbed floors. Anything that would take my attention and tire my muscles.

But now, tonight, this too-wide bed fits two again. The weight beside, that I know is him, doesn't move in the blackness. The blood stalls in my veins; the air in my throat. But I can hold off no longer and I have to allow a small breath out and in, slow and quiet as I can; just a shuddering of diaphragm beneath my nightshirt.

Then, as I'm about to reach out, to touch the raised hill of blanket that must be there, light explodes and yellows the room. I jump and sit up. The lamp that was on when the power went out burns once more. The house alarm see-saws and sees off the quiet.

Then. Beside me.

The blanket drops in waves.

There is no body there now. He is gone.

A spring twangs in the mattress, relieved at his leaving. And next to the bed, the maggot lies dead in the bowl.

Interesting, she says, when I tell her. *Really interesting.*

'Interesting? What's interesting about it?' The words are razors in my throat.

The light and the alarm. Too much too soon.

'You could have warned me…that he could be scared off.'

She sighs. A gust of wind blows leaves from the tree and throws them against the window: a handful of bronze confetti.

It was too much too soon for you, she says. *Not him. It all depends on you and how much you believe it. I told you that.*

I hear the soft chink of ice cube against glass and the woman gulps.

What happened stopped you believing. Simple as that.

The wind pushes the leaves into the corner of the window, trapping them there: its invisible fingertips holding them down. 'Oh,' I say. 'What do I do now?'

Nothing, she says. *You get one go, that's your lot. Sorry.*

I pace the floor and squeeze the phone. Its plastic shell cracks. 'That can't be it,' I say. 'There must be something else.'

No, sorry. It'd be too hard for you now.

But she doesn't hang up. The ice cubes clink faster and I imagine a bony hand swirling the drink until it almost tips out.

'I can send you more money,' I say. 'I can do that.'

She doesn't speak.

'How much do you want? I can send it now.'

I hear her put the glass down and imagine a table ringed with stains and snowy with ash.

OK, she says. There's a low drumming sound; fingers tapping on the arm of a chair. *Make it five.*

'Hundred? Half what it was before?'

The woman laughs and the gritty rattling of her chest starts her coughing and choking. She gulps hard, the ice cubes clicking against her teeth. There's a clatter and the phone is dropped, then a rush of air. After a couple of minutes there's a scuffing over the mouthpiece and deep breaths. *Thousand,* she says, her voice narrowed, as if she's talking through a megaphone. I hear the hiss of oxygen louder now behind her laboured breathing.

'Are you OK?' I ask.

Five thousand, she says. *And then I'll tell you what to do.*

Outside the wind drops and the leaves fall from the windowsill. The garden bruises over from the pressing in of clouds.

I clean out my savings and hug the money to me before I send it to the P. O. Box. The day after I phone her again. Her breaths are ragged. More of them weed up into her sentences.

This time what I am to use will not be my choice. It will be hers.

It would have been better if it'd worked the first time, she says, tutting. *It gets harder the longer it goes on. You have to do more.*

'More?' I ask, my pen over the paper, awaiting instruction.

Look, I know you want it, but it's the believing that gets harder. She pauses. *When you start feeling he's really gone, you might as well forget it. That's why.* She clears her throat. *Doing more helps you to believe more.*

In the time since that day I have refused to dwell on it – his face pressed to the carpet in his study, glasses broken from the impact of his fall from the chair; one hand touching the place where his heart had been beating. I have held my hand up at this memory for weeks but now it barges its way in and makes me see it.

'Oh,' I say and touch my throat. I push the thought away.

See, she says. *It's getting more difficult by the minute.*

This time I have to get a cat and a freshly dead mouse. And I must use water.

I buy a white, shivering mouse from the pet shop, set a trap with cheese and lock them both in the kitchen until I hear the metallic jaw snap. I run the bath and put its broken body at the bottom, blocking out what I've done. Then in the early hours I tempt next door's cat in with 'chu-chu's and a plate of tuna. Once inside I get it by the scruff and hold it out at arm's length, avoiding its claws and trying not to hear its hisses.

In the bathroom I kneel on the tiles and make new sounds, off-key sounds, pinning the cat down with its wails and glinting eyes. When the movement starts, the animal falls quiet, and this time the vibrations get stronger, faster. When the room shakes so much that I think I'm going to vomit, I lift and plunge the cat into the bath. Releasing it when its body touches the bottom. Water lurching up my arm and onto the floor.

I carry on with the sounds and the cat splashes and swims up, its wet head surfacing like a furred buoy. It scrambles and claws at the bath until it is up and over the side, skidding for the door. The ritual ends and the vibrations stop. I run downstairs after it, to let it out. The back door swings, its hinges squeaking, but I can't see it. I grasp the door and look out into the darkness but there is no sign of it. I lock doors and switch off lights, release the water and flush the mouse. In bed I twist the blanket in my hands, and then pull it around me, until I am caught up in its rough knots.

'Is it you?'

The voice is low, no louder than a whisper. But electronic. A computer voice.

I have been lying with my eyes closed. But now they open wide and wild and fix themselves on the brightening ceiling.

'Is it you?' It comes again, from in the bed beside me.

'Oh, Christ,' I say, without knowing I'm saying it. 'Oh, my Christ.'

'Woman,' it says, monotone, and I know it's him. This was his joke.

I turn, slow, afraid it's my imagination, but there he is; facing me. The blanket pulled up over his head, his eyes black coins – the electric blue irises, gone. I try to drag my hands from the blanket.

'Don't touch me,' he says.

Water blurs my vision. I blink it away.

'I'm not here yet,' he says, the voice humanising. 'It takes a while.'

I shiver all over as if I am both cold and hot at the same time: my body a current of charged liquid. 'Christ,' I say.

A smile appears in the shadows of his face. 'No, just me.' The electronic tones have almost gone from his voice.

I laugh and cry, water rolling from my eyes and mixing with the patch of damp I can feel beneath my nose. 'I can't believe it.'

He flickers like a television that's not properly tuned in and there's a buzzing sound as he does so. I lift my hand to my mouth.

'Don't say that,' he says, then smiles again. 'Please.'

'Oh, no.' My breath hot on my palm. 'I believe, of

course I believe. It's just…amazing.'

He pulls the blanket further over his head. 'Cold,' he says, shivering. 'But not for much longer.'

My neck begins to ache from keeping it raised up from the pillow as I look at him. I let my head fall and the pain softens and fades. 'Why are you…? Where have you…?'

He puts a finger to his lips. 'Not yet.'

Tears continue to build and fall and I carry on watching him as colour blooms in his face. Only the black eyes remain. I wonder if he will still need his glasses but then I remember that they're broken. We will have to buy him new ones.

Just as I'm thinking this there's a movement at the bottom of the bed. His eyes widen but he doesn't speak. I raise my head to see if he's kicked a leg out of bed as he always did whenever he was too warm. But I look down and it isn't his leg. It's next door's cat. Its body stiff, eyes fixed on the risen bedclothes. It hisses, makes its wailing sound. The air curdles and thickens around us. It opens its mouth wider and hisses again, this time louder and longer.

'Away,' he says, monotone, electronic again.

I move my foot to try and tip the cat from the bed but it holds firm. It just stares at him and growls.

'Away,' he says again, and flickers. Buzzing fills the room.

I kick at the cat and it claws at my foot. 'Get out.' I slip my toes beneath it and throw it from the bed. It lands with a thump on the floor.

It leaps up onto the windowsill and skitters out through the open window. I get out of bed and run over, expecting to see it dead in the grass below. But instead it is running through a gap in the hedge that separates the gardens, its body unhurt.

Something about the angle of my head, staring down, feeling myself standing over the possibility of death, returns me to that moment of finding him in his study. Looking at his still body, his pale lips parted but no air passing through. I clench my fists as I remember pushing at his heart with the heels of my hands, but nothing re-igniting. Pressing and pressing until something cracked and gave way beneath them; the noise opening something up inside my head – a buried pathway that had always been there, becoming, at that moment, floodlit with harsh light.

I turn back to the bed. He is flickering more now. And creasing up his eyes with each surge as he shifts from grey to colour, colour to grey. The buzzing is everywhere, as if each molecule of air is alive with it.

'No,' I say and lean towards him, across the bed.

'Sorry,' he says, and all at once he is just a human outline filled in with TV snow.

'Please,' I say, reaching.

'I can't –'

'Don't go.'

'– stay,' he says.

'No,' I shout.

And the blanket falls. The buzzing stops.

I swipe my hands over where he had been lying, feeling for something – anything – real; some remnant to grab and claim as mine, to use as part of some new ritual and bring him back again. But there is nothing. Nothing but wrinkled sheets and the squashed pillow.

Everything tightens within me and I fall on the bed; smell the blanket and the sheets but there is only the scent of chemical flowers from the wash powder.

I breathe in and make the sounds again. My voice loud and raw. I do this for a long time. Repeating the cycle of sounds over and over. But the vibrations don't return. The room is still.

And the membrane between our two worlds grows thicker.

I dial the woman's number, my fingers trembling over the buttons. It rings. Three times, four times. I hold on. Eleven times and then the answerphone. It's a standard message from the phone company. Not the woman or even the man I once heard who I presume is her husband. Just an automated woman whose message has been stitched together by an operator or a computer programme into a patchwork of words.

I hang up and phone again. On the fifth ring, a man's voice.

'Hello?'

I grip the receiver; my mind empties out.

'Hello?' he says again.

I take a deep breath. 'Is she there?' I say. I never knew her name.

'She?' he says.

'The woman,' I say. 'I phoned her a few times. She told me what to do.'

The television is turned up loud where he is. The presenter is giving directions to the empty room behind him – saying how to make a Sunday roast: goose fat for the roast potatoes, fresh breadcrumbs and sage for the stuffing that will go inside the chicken's cavity.

'Lydia? She's gone,' he says, each word clipped short. 'Yesterday.'

The presenter is firmer, stressing that if people follow her guidelines strictly – especially the timings and the heat settings – then the meal will be perfect. Flawless.

'Who is this?' he asks, his voice sour.

I put a hand to the back of my head and cradle it.

'Did she leave any information? Any instructions on what to do?'

The television is silenced. 'Instructions? For what?'

'She must have left something,' I say. 'Maybe written down somewhere?'

'What are you talking about? Who is this?'

'I need to do another ritual…or whatever she called it,' I say. I tug the hair at the back of my head until my scalp burns. 'I can send you money if that's what you want. Or if it's not money, something else – I'll do anything.'

'Ritual?' he says. 'Look, I think you have the wrong number. You must want somebody else.'

'No,' I say. 'It's definitely this number. I got it from a friend of a friend. Please.'

'I'm sorry,' he says. 'Please don't ring here again.'

The line goes dead.

I phone back. He picks up but doesn't speak. When I say 'hello' he puts the phone down. When I try again it just rings and rings and goes to the answerphone. And when I ring once more it does the same.

All night I lie awake. At four in the morning when I try again, there's a message.

'The number you have dialled has not been recognised. Please hang up and try again.'

I press the buttons, knowing the man couldn't have had the line cut so quickly.

'The number you have dialled has not been recognised. Please hang up…'

I put my finger over the zero, ready to begin again. If I believe I can get through I will get through. I force myself to believe. I press the zero and in my head I am on the floodlit path. I press the next number and take a step along it: the light goes out behind me. Something falls like dandruff.

I press and take another step. I don't know where the path leads.

With each number, another step and a light goes out. I can't stop myself now.

At the last number I am on the final step. I wait then press the seven. The light fails. I am now in darkness, both behind and in front. There are no more lights left to come on.

I wait for the words.

They do not come.

In my mind I feel myself bend down and feel on the path, trying to gather up whatever it is that has fallen from me. But there are too many gaps between my fingers to keep hold of it.

Then.

'The number you have dialled has not been recognised. Please hang up and try again.'

Michael Coleman

The Bedroom

The curtain dimmed bedroom was still and peaceful – like a convent chapel. The silence was nearly joyful, but there would be no joy in this room again – not for us.

This was her room. I had always just called it the bedroom – she had always called it her bedroom, as in "Be nice to me or I might not allow you into my bedroom tonight." She often called it the heart of the family because, "this is where we made them all."

Together we had over the years changed it to suit our tastes and needs for a particular time. But it was definitely her room. She had more drawers, and more wardrobe space than me, and she had nearly all the surface space. Me – I was just happy to share it with her. I would have shared anything to be with her.

She had bewitched me when she was just sixteen, casting her spell naturally and innocently – just by being her, no pretend coyness, nor awkward teenage flirting – she was just so pretty and so nice. And I had remained gladly spellbound for every one of the forty years since. No matter about all our ups and downs – that spell never broke. Her being the mother of my four children never stopped her from just being – my girl.

In my mind's eye she would always be a sixteen year old beauty with plaits.

Now as I sadly gazed down on her asleep it looked as if the big bed was starting to devour her. It was all fluffy-white and plump – and she had grown so tiny and thin. My dying little angel was now helplessly captured by her own betraying body in the bed's cloudlike folds.

*

God – we had some times here – scarlet fun-filled

nights. Candles in red glass. Exotic nights. Entwined shadows, huge and flickering on the patterned walls – so alive, so bold. Musky perfume. Dark music. The room throbbed with heightened senses and expectations. Our own Hellfire Club, here in the bedroom. For a few hours we would be the pulsating, absolute centre of our own universe. No thought of work, or children, or the exploding, life threatening Belfast streets. This room was a retreat, a haven – no, it was more than that. It was a kingdom. That's what we had done, we had built a kingdom in this house, the kingdom of our life together, and this room was its epicentre- the throne room.

What I wouldn't give for one more of those nights. For our kingdom back again. To worship my queen.

Our wonderful normality was now being cruelly extracted from us – through her. Cell by dying cell, layer by fading layer. Each day more of her life escaped through the pale translucent skin. Her gleaming emerald eyes were now like beach glass. Though a hint of the colour was still there, beneath the frosted surface their mischief and sparkling promise was gone – forever. We were losing our kingdom with every small breath she managed to steal from the begrudging air.

Why? Why us?

Oh! Thundering anger here you come again. Rumbling through me. Shaking my legs. Twisting the muscles in my neck until they curl pain, like a breaking wave, right across my head. I chased it away; today there must be no anger. I had learned to control this resentful anger now – because I did not have the time for it. I had had important tending and loving to do these past months.

My panic was different from my flashes of anger. Though I also managed to I keep it in check it had been constant for all these months. Minute after minute it cracked and growled within me. Like pack ice – it was constantly shoving and moving, yet going nowhere – waiting for a destructive thaw which would be its only release. The pandemonium wanted to burst through and find release. Our world was disappearing and I had no response. Defeat was imminent. And I was powerless, hopelessly powerless. But in front of her I had kept the panic and the anger hidden. That is what we all do in a situation like this. We try, with a veneer of a smile and a feeble light-heartedness to plead ignorance to the awful truth, making a show of normality – for their sake – the sufferer, the victim, the soon to be dead loved one. And all this pretence is useless, for they know, only too well, the deadly inevitable truth. Because it has been mercilessly thrust upon them. Deep into their very being. It has invaded and become part of the essence of who they now are – their death was conceived at this truth's birth, and now like two deadly twins they are bound together in a journey to joint oblivion.

*

Her little breaths murmured a mantra into the peacefulness of the room, they were like a little pulse just below the silence. Their rhythm and the afternoon light, soft and embracing through the curtains, gently drew me to her. I lay down on top of the covers beside her and held her waning little hand.

We were always one in this small space.

I stared as if in a trance at the white ceiling and then drifted through it to some distant, thought chasing nothingness.

My love, my love, where are you going?

What about us?

What about me?

Christ, what about me? A huge, expansive void was about to fill this small space. I knew it was going to crush me, like starlight sucked into a black hole. And the ensuing darkness would be forever. There would never be light in my life again.

She would call me selfish for these selfish thoughts. She used to call me selfish on weekend mornings because I would yell at the four kids to go into their own rooms and leave us to sleep. The echoes of their young voices and those boisterous attacks on our bed, leading to mass family tickling fights, would forever be part of our history in this room. Like the layers of wallpaper on the wall behind the wardrobe. I had always left a patch of the old paper there, under each new pattern – a hidden archive of our time here. I know that one day some stranger will surely steam and scrape it thoughtlessly away. Like us it will disappear.

*

They had all been weaned in this room. In a Moses basket that always sat at my side of the bed. Sleepless nights and teething gel. Bottle warmers, nappy pins, the smell of baby sick and talcum powder – all the consequence of too many red-perfumed nights. An uninvited little smile came with that thought. Although she was lying here beside me, and I was holding her hand, it was the loneliest smile in the world.

As they got older they were nursed here when sick, or sheltered between us from bad dreams. If I was half asleep I just hooked out an arm when one of them appeared at my head and scooped them up and over and down into the warmth between us. Like an old steam express grabbing a hung mailbag from the trackside and throwing it safely into the guard's carriage.

The twins had been born here – in this very room. That was a night. She thought it was cramps at first because she was not due until the following week. They came so easy. Just two strangers – slipping from the unknown – into our lives. When we realised they were on their way I called an ambulance, but they were crying with hunger on the bed, wrapped in two big towels, their cords still attached, by the time it arrived. The other two were hopping about between their room and ours as it was happening. Excited and scared, they giggled and hushed, and then giggled again as things unfolded. I was terrified, but she was calm and motherly through it all, calling out to the gigglers "Don't worry Daddy knows what he's doing." And winked at me with those luscious, teasing green eyes.

"This is your fault you know. You should leave me alone at night." She breathlessly laughed as she rode another contraction. She was always good with pain.

Now they were all off – building their own kingdoms. Their lives now grey and darkened by her illness. Today's plan had been emotionally disclosed to them – there was little discussion however. They all objected – saying the views of all the family had to be listened to, that we had to hope and pray for a miracle She was not strong enough to argue that she had lost all hope, that she could no longer go on, so I just put my arm around her and explained that in this situation we were a family of two. This was our business – like planning a family – this was just between her and me. They knew I was talking for her, and with a heart more broken than theirs. Their love for us both filled the room as they quietly accepted the inevitability of what was to come – we all cried gently together – as only a family can do at a time like this.

*

It had just been the two of us there when the doctor told us how sick she would become – and that nothing could be done for her. We came home and we lay for hours on this bed. Shocked, our thoughts churned in isolated silence. So close, yet barely touching each other. Part of me wanted to blame her for this affliction on our lives. She had brought this into our lives not me. My anger wanted to blame somebody, but of course how could I blame her. There was nobody to blame. And that only made it worse, this heartbreaking waste. No one had sent this as a judgement, a punishment – it was cruel fate – bad luck. So we just lay there – numbed. It was as if we had had a row. Like one of those times when a bed seems as wide as an ocean and two people lie – like immovable continents – a storm raging on the cotton sea between them.

That day drifted slowly away and the room became dark and cold.

So we got up and ate. We then tried to talk as we stared across the table at each other, but each time we tried one of us would start to weep. We drank wine, and smoked an old, dried up joint I knew had been lurking for a long time in the corner of a drawer. That night we fumbled a failed passion as we searched for an anchor, for the old secure reality – it had always been our safest retreat. God, we thought it would go on forever.

But now we had a new and broken world – nothing would ever be the same.

*

I could have died for her the first time she soiled the bed. Her pain was burden enough, but this I knew was her big cross. The complete unpleasantness of it was deeply alien and shocking to her. She did not look at me as I cleaned the bed and her up. "Don't worry. This is easy. I can do this my love." I told her, my words awash with all the compassion and love I felt for her in that moment.

She did not lift her head from where it fallen onto her raised knees, her arms clasping her legs and her hair hanging limply down over them as she replied "I cannot." Her voice was flat and beaten – yet her words were certain.

Those two words went to my heart like a dagger. I knew what they meant.

She could not speak to me, nor look at me for another two days, such was the shame she felt at her helplessness.

It was inevitable what was to follow.

*

Many times in the past we had sat and discussed the meaning of life – and death – and sin – and God. Easy discussions with a glass of wine in your hand, and a smug faith in your own continuing good fortune.

I was not sure about God – she was sure, she believed. In spite of this I was not sure about taking life, even early abortion – but she could see justified occasions for all such drastic and controversial acts. We would end these abstract discussions casually – each of us sure of our own position, and comfortable in the knowledge we would surely never have these positions tested. Poor human fools.

One night as I propped the pillows behind her for her to sit up and take some medicine, she affectionately stroked my face – and beginning to cry she said. "You love me – deeply. Into your very bones. I know this, deep into my bones. And I know you believe in hope. But I cannot. I cannot hope when I hurt like I do – and it is getting worse. I cannot hope when I know what I know. I cannot hope as I feel myself fading away. I cannot hope when you have to clean me like a baby. There is no hope my love. It will be over within months. But I cannot endure this all for months. Please, please, love me well and release me from all this. Please."

She had said it. I knew it was coming. Then my poor love cradled my head in those sick, skinny arms as I sobbed hopelessly into her impoverished hair. She knew I could not refuse her. Later as I battled my despairing mind I tortured myself with the thought she was being selfish by asking for this, after all, she knew I would not refuse her. But really I knew she was desperate and had no where else to turn. In the end this was not about the kids, it was not about society or the moral judgements of others. This was about our life, the one we had made, the life that we owned together, unlike the drawer space in this room this one life was built on the total equality of our relationship, on our love and our respect for each other. Only God, or one of us could end it. And I believed both her and I had more rights here than God.

*

And so now, throughout this morning, I had fed her medicine and tablets, lots of tablets. She asked for some wine, why not we thought. But not too much in case she became so sick as to bring the tablets back up – that would complicate everything. God, we were being so scientific and practical. She smiled a lot, and we touched a lot. We whispered our love to each other, and talked of how we had met, and how lucky we were to have had this time given to us out of the infinite eternity of existence, and how wonderful our children were. I held and stroked her, continuing to gently talk to her as at last she fell into this, her most untroubled sleep for such a long time. I knew we would never speak again – Jesus this cannot be real, this is just not happening. But it was. This was happening to us. How can we never speak again? How can this be?

Oh! God! Help us. Help me.

I set her hand back down on the soft quilt and turned to look at her. She was breathing so softly, wherever she was now she was certainly not in pain. I had not seen her look so peaceful for months, and the loveliness of her face was there, delicately taut over her jaw and cheek bones, and even a little colour in her cheeks – red wine always did that to her, flaming her face, she hated it when that happened. I knew I could not let her come back – I loved her too much. I could not let her down. She knew she could always rely on me and that I would never fail her. I cupped her head in my hands and kissed her lips – they felt cool – but as soft and yielding as ever, even now a flare of our passion briefly came over me. Judas.

He too had sealed his betrayal with a kiss. But no this was not a betrayal – this was her wish. Perhaps it had been Jesus's wish also? Was I Judas?

I felt more like a God as I clasped my pillow to my chest and rolled onto her.

I pressed the pillow, as gently as I could, over the

face I had loved all my adult life.

Suddenly in the midst of this horror I remembered a day in 1972 – we had been caught up in one of those impromptu Belfast gun battles. The IRA at one corner, the British Army at the other, and us caught in the middle. I had pushed her to the ground and lay right over her as the bullets screamed above and around us. I did not heed her words. "You're smothering me. I can't breathe" as I pressed her closer into the ground. I would have taken every bullet that came down the street just so I could protect her.

And now I was smothering her again.

My body was shaking. I felt her going. Her soul passed through me. Touching every cell in my body. Into and right through my trembling heart – tearing it asunder – and out into the ether, to the unknown. Leaving me forever. I screamed a long anguished cry into the cold, empty room. The room in which we had conceived and birthed life. Now together we had ended life here. Our throne room was now a bitter and sour place – desecrated. Some time later I rolled off her.

I took her small lifeless hand and held it tight.

I stared through the ceiling into nothingness. I cared for nothing. I was nothing.

The day drifted slowly out of the room, and it and my darling became cold.

David Frankel

The Place

I was a young man when I found The Place. It happened when Mother was still alive, but apart from that things were much the same as they are now. I still live in the house I was raised in; a great Victorian terrace on the edge of a town that I have never seen. My parents were advanced in years when I was born and Father died when I was a young child so my memories of him are vague. I only really felt his presence when I worked in the garden using the tools that he left behind in the garden shed where the air was warm and smelled of soil. Each had its own place, meticulously kept; hanging on the wall and each had its handle worn smooth by his hand, any traces of varnish or paint long since gone. Apart from his tools and the money that kept Mother and I, he left only a set of detailed gardening diaries that described in detail every task he had performed, with notes about each plant he had nurtured. He grew old before his time and was never able to teach me what he knew. It was from his fastidious records that I learned everything I needed to look after the house and the garden. The detail and length of the entries tailed off towards the end but I had already been well trained; I was very young when I first began pushing the lawn mower around and learned how to repair roof felt. I can remember when the garden became overgrown and things began to slowly fall apart while my father sat in his chair looking out of the window through half closed eyes.

The diaries contained much more than his thorough records on how to nurture the garden. Small comments and notes in the margins gave away signs of the man that had written the entries, and there were other things in the diaries I never discussed with Mother. Things I knew she must never find out. The father I remembered was not the quiet man in a chair but a man I'd constructed from lines in notebooks.

I've never had a job. By the time my brief and sporadic school career had petered out mother needed me to look after the house and its expanse of garden. Following the guiding words that Father had left, I divided my time between maintaining the echoing rooms with their high ceilings, and growing vegetables and flowers in the gardens. Mother used to call me her estate manager. According to her I'd inherited both my father's green fingers and his dirty fingernails.

What I couldn't grow we bought from the grocer's store in the row of shops where I took Mother once a week. While she shopped for groceries I'd browse in the tiny ironmongers shop or occasionally buy clothes from the tailors. I usually went in alone because Mother trusted me to buy something respectable; I always try to look smart, so I like to wear a shirt at all times, old ones for gardening. In the photographs I have of father he always has a shirt on. He would've liked to know I wasn't letting standards slip. Next to the shops is a library. Mother disliked having books in the house because they collect dust, but I like to read so I often went there when mother was snoozing in the afternoon, transported to her own world by music on the radio, and later I would sit with a cup of milky tea and read, keeping her company while she stood ironing in the kitchen, the air filled with the smell of warm cotton. She would pause only to tut at dirt that her cheap brand of detergent had failed to remove from my gardening shirts. Aside from this, the only noise was the dull thud of the iron on the padded board and the quiet clicking of the iron's thermostat.

I remember exactly when I found The Place. It was a strange, unsettling time. It was shortly before my thirtieth birthday and I had just met Marianne for the first time. She was the niece of Mrs Landy who'd recently replaced our aged neighbour, Mr. Baron. He'd lived next door since before I was born. Mother disliked Mrs Landy and her family immediately. She disliked change of any kind but spoke about them as though they'd driven the old man into the nursing home themselves and stolen his house from under him. When a satellite dish appeared on the front of their house she said it was a clear sign that the neighbourhood was going to the dogs. Not that we were old fashioned; we'd had a television since I was quite young. In any case, I was instructed to 'maintain a polite distance' from them.

The first time Marianne spoke to me I couldn't see her. I was weeding the borders and singing to myself when I heard somebody in the next garden say 'Hello. Lovely day isn't it?' Not realising it was directed at me, I went on with my weeding. When the voice persisted I asked, as politely as I could, if she was talking to me. 'Who do you think I'm talkin' to? I've said hello three bleedin' times.' Although she was pretending to be angry, I could tell that beyond the wall she was smiling. I introduced myself and told her that I lived with Mother, and she said 'That's nice.' We had a very nice conversation about the weather before I said goodbye and went indoors. I hadn't finished what I was doing but I couldn't think of anything else to say to her and I wasn't sure what else to do. I left my tools and the weeds I'd pulled up in a pile on the lawn so I had to go back out that evening and tidy up.

Two days later I was working in the garden, near a spot where the roots from fruit trees that grow in both gardens intertwined and bulged up from the ground, breaking through the soil and undermining the wall, causing its partial collapse. Movement beyond the tumble of masonry caught my eye and I realised immediately that it was Marianne. It was the first time I'd seen her. She was wearing men's clothes, dirty from gardening. I couldn't help staring; comparing her to the picture of her I'd constructed from the sound of her voice. She saw me watching her and I looked away embarrassed. To my surprise she approached the wall and drew a cigarette from a packet in her shirt pocket. I think another reason mother hated Mrs Landy, aside from being new to the area and having a satellite dish, was that her whole family smoked. I carried on with what I was doing but when I glanced up she was still standing there smoking.

'Hello again Lenny.'

I said hello and went over to the wall.

'I'm guessing you don't smoke Lenny,' she said holding the packet out to me doubtfully. I don't know how she could tell by looking at me but I shook my head and thanked her, smiling to be polite.

'Father smoked a pipe,' I said, unsure of what else to say, never having been offered a cigarette before.

She ignored me and carried on, 'Sorry about the other day. I bet you thought I was a nutter or something?' she said.

'No, I didn't think that at all.'

'What did you think then?' she asked smiling.

Again, I was in uncharted waters; 'I thought you had a lovely voice,' I said honestly.

She laughed, 'This voice came courtesy of Benson and Hedges.'

I was worried that mother would be watching me from the house. We were hidden from view by the foliage on boughs that were weighed down by small hard apples, but I still wanted to bring the conversation to an end; 'Doesn't your aunt worry about you talking to strange men down the garden?'

But she said 'A bloke who puts a clean shirt on to dig the flower beds must be respectable Lenny,' and carried on talking. If I'm honest, I didn't listen to a lot of what she said that first day. A mixture of excitement and fascination made it difficult to concentrate. I could never think of the right things to say when I talked to people so I found it relaxing that she didn't mind talking while I was quiet, although sometimes her directness was unnerving.

We talked, or rather she talked, for a long time. I learned, among a great many other things, that her aunt was paying her to clear the badly overgrown garden. She was killing time before going to university at the end of summer. I suppose it was natural for her to ask what I did, but when I told her she seemed amazed; 'Don't you ever want a job or to go to college?'

'I didn't go to school. I can't do anything.' Perhaps for the first time this seemed wrong and I found myself worrying about what she'd think of me.

'How come you didn't go to school Lenny?'

'Well, I did, but not for long. Mother said it was because I noticed too much and learned too little, and it got me into trouble.' I laughed but she just looked confused so I stopped and said 'I was just no good at it I suppose.' Going to school used to frighten me too, but I wasn't going to tell Marianne that.

We spoke very often after that day. We were both out in the garden a lot, and I admit that I spent more time out there than I should've that summer. When I mentioned Marianne to mother she said 'Stay away from her. She's a tart. All hair and make up.' Mother was obviously keeping a close eye on Mrs Landy and her niece, treating them with a suspicion beyond that which she usually held for new people moving into the area, so I didn't speak to Mother about Marianne again.

If I was in the garden I always made sure my hair was combed and my shirt was clean.

It was days later, my mind still full of Marianne, that I found The Place. Since my early childhood I've known every inch of the garden: My parents, always mistrustful of the world, didn't allow me to go beyond its walls and it hasn't changed very much since then. An expanse of lawn, hemmed in by rambling borders, gives way to a sparse vegetable garden and unruly fruit trees. At the far end, beyond the slowly collapsing hulk of a disused shed is an expanse of wilderness where, as a child, I lived out my fantasies and build my own kingdoms.

That was where I found it. At the very end of the garden where the soil was sour and black from years of neglect and garden fires had left scorched irregular patches on the ground. Brambles spread reluctantly, searching for light in the almost constant shade of a horse-chestnut tree that grew in one of the gardens beyond our own, and this small forgotten patch of ground was surrounded on three sides by the boundary wall, its bricks softened by age and forced apart by advancing creepers. It was a brilliant morning and I was clearing undergrowth at the bottom of the garden. My attempts to remove the creepers by hand had only been partially successful so I began to scrape the wall with the blade of my father's spade sending a flow of crumbling mortar down the face of the brickwork along with the coils of creeper. Without warning the end of the spade disappeared into the wall pitching me forward onto my knees. I knelt on the trampled weeds for a moment looking for a hole where I expected the brickwork had given way. I was confused to find the wall appeared solid. Picking up the spade I poked once more at the wall only to see the blade disappear without resistance into what appeared to be solid brickwork. I regained my footing and stood for a moment, unsure of what to do and unable to reconcile what I could see with what had happened. As the shock wore off, my curiosity grew. I crouched closer to the wall to watch more closely as I pushed the spade forward once again. Scrutinised from a few inches away, there was no doubt that what I had seen was true. The spade passed into the wall disappearing as though it were being dipped into an opaque fluid. Overwhelmed by sudden fear I flung myself back, dropping the spade which struck the paving stones of the garden path with a reassuringly solid clunk.

I don't know how long I stared at the wall while I struggled to regain my composure, but when I finally stood again my legs were stiff from inaction. I thrust the spade into the wall still expecting it to meet resistance, but there was none. It disappeared up to handle. Leaving it in place I scrambled to look over the wall which was no more than twelve inches deep. There was no sign of anything projecting on the other side. Reaching down I pulled an old fence post out of the ground and used it to strike the back of the wall. I pounded the bricks until the vibrations hurt my arm, but it was solid. By moving the spade from side to side I was able to find out that the place I'd discovered was a little more than three bricks wide and four high. Its edges seemed firm but not hard. I began to throw small stones and twigs at it, watching them disappear soundlessly into the bricks. It was almost dark by the time I'd summoned the courage to touch it. Infinitely slowly, I placed my rigid hand into the wall. I experienced no sensation at all, as though there were nothing there. I was almost unable to comprehend the image of my hand submerged in masonry. Fear fought excitement as my arm passed the elbow and then as my shoulder neared the threshold I felt the same definite but soft resistance that the spade had met. Not wet or dry, warm or cold, hard or soft. The edges, if you could call them that, were formed by an increasing resistance like a thickening liquid that first became dough-like and then thicker still until it was impossible to press any further. Moving my hand around inside the space I was able to find the projectiles I had thrown in. My finger tips closed around a pebble and I pulled it back out and stared at it. Squinting in the failing light, I felt as though I was holding a jewel.

I wondered for a long time what it was for and if I should tell anyone. I can't explain why I didn't except that I honestly don't think anyone would have believed me. People are always polite but I know they think I'm not right in the head, and how would I have told tell them anyway; I didn't even know how to describe what I'd seen. I wasn't sure what mother would make of it, and I didn't want to telephone the council in case they took it away. It didn't seem to be hurting anyone so I decided to keep it and continue my observations and experiments. In the days that followed I tried to find out more about it, but all the words in all the science books in the library yielded nothing. I couldn't find references to anything like it. In desperation I tried the books on the 'supernatural and mysteries' shelf but there was nothing there either.

I'm good at keeping things to myself. I never told Mother or anyone else about the neatly folded letters in Father's diaries, each one written in neat blue ink on pale blue paper. They were addressed to my father at his office in town, all from a lady called Sandra and dated in 1962; the year I was born. They had been safe for all those years, between the pages of the diaries, where only I could take them out and read them. I had kept them secret and would keep The Place secret.

After cleaning and packing away my father's tools, I went indoors, washed and came down for tea as I always did, eating in silence while mother talked. She knew something was amiss. 'Have you spoken to the neighbours today Leonard? You were outside a very long time.' She meant Marianne. I couldn't speak: After what I'd seen, the conversation seemed trivial. She took my silence as an admission of some indiscretion. 'What would your dear father have said Leonard?' As she gathered the dinner plates she reminded me, as she frequently did, how the event of my birth had weakened her fragile constitution, how popular she had been before motherhood had ruined her natural good looks, and she finished as she always did '…but your father wanted you very, very much.' I wondered, if this was true, what the letters I'd found in his diaries had meant. When Sandra had written to my father about my upcoming birth she told him 'I know this isn't what we wanted but you have to stay now, and I understand. Enid needs you.' I remember it precisely because it seemed so strange seeing Mother referred to by her first name instead of Mrs Smart or just 'Mother'. I used to wonder how well Sandra knew her.

In one of the letters was a picture of Sandra. She had a kind, pretty face and in the old fashioned formal pose she looked too polite to have said some of the things she had written to my father. From the picture I could imagine her voice, like Marianne's, speaking the words she had written. I liked to read them; they described another world where my father was a heroic figure, important and well travelled. A world different from the one I knew. I loved mother but it was nice to know that Father had another friend.

I went to my room early that night but couldn't

sleep. I lay in my bed, the same bed I had slept in since I was a boy, wide awake until I gave up trying to sleep and sat against the wall where I could look out of the window. I peered into the darkness at the bottom of the garden, looking for any change; anything else in the world that had become different.

The next morning I ignored Mother's questions. I went directly down the garden where I spent the morning repeating my experiments of the previous day, to reassure myself that I wasn't losing my mind (on my long night watch I had begun to suspect hallucination). Later, with the results confirmed, I sat on the floor leaning my back against the dilapidated shed, staring at the bricks with their invisible secret. I tried placing different objects into it and even one or two insects I found beneath the undergrowth. All came out unaffected by their experience. The place was completely unchanged from the previous day, and I decided that whatever it was and whatever caused it, it was there to stay.

From where I sat with my back to the creosote stained wood, I was able to see into the neighbouring garden through the gap beneath the apple trees. Absorbed as I had been, I hadn't noticed that Marianne was there, hacking through the bushes and towering weeds that dominated the Landy's side of the wall. I could see she'd been struggling to hack through some of the trunks. I'd been sitting so quietly that she hadn't noticed I was there so, unusually, it was me that spoke first. When I asked if she would like some help trimming her bush, she laughed and held the saw out to me. I climbed over wall loosening some flints and I had to scramble to keep my balance, stumbling into her as she stepped forward to help me. Regaining my footing I felt the softness of her breast press against my arm. The smell of her perfume cut through the heavier smell of earth and torn plants and I felt myself blush deeply. The tension was broken by Mrs Landy shouting down the garden; 'Marianne?'

She shouted back raucously, 'Hello aunty. I'm just talking to Lenny from next door.' I peered through the trees to see Mrs Landy looking down the garden curiously. I waved, unsure of myself, silently desperate for Marianne to stop shouting in case Mother should hear.

'Hello Lenny love. How's your mum?'

Before I could answer, Marianne said sniggering, 'Lenny said he'd come over and trim your bush.' Mrs Landy waved her away and retreated to the house shaking her head.

I took the saw from Marianne and hacked into the bushes, sawing as fast as I could, worried that Mother had heard Mrs Landy. When the biggest of the shrubs were down and cut into manageable sections I said 'I'd better get back. Mother will be wondering what I am up to.' I thought of the tall windows of the back parlour: Gunmetal slabs of glass from where mother could survey the garden.

'She keeps you on a short rein your mum don't she?'

'She just worries about me.'

'Worries about the company you're keeping does she? Don't she like me?'

I didn't know what to say. 'I don't think mother likes your satellite dish,' I laughed in case she was offended.

'What's the matter with that? Don't she like telly?' she asked with one hand on her hip.

'Not much. She thinks there's too much smut and violence on.'

'And what do you think? She's only half right, I bet,'

she laughed. I laughed with her, but I wasn't really sure why. That happened a lot when I was talking to Marianne. She found a lot of things funny. That was one of the things I liked about her. There was a kind of lightness in her that the people I knew around here didn't have. She was like an actress from an old film, but plumper. After that I thought about her a lot. I thought about the place a lot too. Each night I'd sit on my window sill and watch the end of the garden. In the daylight, tired, I'd sit and watch The Place while the weeds grew unchecked.

The first use I found for it was prompted by Mother. Since Marianne's arrival I had noticed Mother taking a keener interest in my activities, even accompanying me to library on one of my visits (I had taken to going to the library almost every day to conduct research). On another occasion I could tell she had been in my room while I was out; the shirts in my cupboard weren't in the same order that I had left them. The only thing I had to hide from her were my father's letters and I began to fear they were no longer safe pressed between the old seed packets and cuttings from gardening magazines that had kept them hidden for thirty years; I knew that mother must never see them but I couldn't bring myself to destroy them. If anything they meant even more to me since I had met Marianne. The words in them made more sense and I would read them while I watched over my discovery from my window each night. Early one morning, while mother was still preparing breakfast, I took the letters carefully wrapped in brown paper, and put them in The Place, where I knew nobody could ever find them.

In my memory, Sandra and Marianne have almost become one identical but even then if I closed my eyes and pictured Sandra she looked a little like Marianne. In the photograph I had of Sandra she was around Marianne's age. We got along well even though I was much older than she was. She only ever mentioned it once:

'How old are you Lenny?'

'I was thirty last week.'

'Oh yeah? You kept that quiet.' She smiled, 'Did you 'ave a party?'

'Yes. My uncle came over and Mother baked some very nice cakes.' She looked at me with an expression I couldn't place and after a long pause she said seriously, 'Well 'appy birthday for last week Lenny.' Three days later she gave me a new trowel badly wrapped in coloured paper and bound with tape. As she leaned over the wall to pass it to me she gave me a kiss on the cheek. I felt my face redden as I thanked her. 'I didn't know what else to get you, and you are always using that old thing.' She went before I could say anything, shouting 'See ya later' over her shoulder. The handle was painted bright yellow and I could see at once that it was from the local hardware shop. It was cheap and poorly made, actually much inferior to my father's old one that lay forgotten at my feet. Afterwards, I kept her gift hidden in the shed, using it only when I could be sure mother wasn't around.

Marianne didn't like my mother any more than Mother liked her. She told me once that I should 'Cut the old apron strings and go and see the world.' She liked to travel and we, or rather she, talked about it a lot. I liked the sound of Australia but the thought of it scared me a bit too. It's funny how even an idea can make you feel afraid. We both knew I'd never go and sometimes I sensed that this annoyed her. Once in particular. She let her hair down and fidgeted with it as we talked and her voice grew harder. 'Why don't you have a gap year from all this. The garden will still be here when you get back, and your mum can look after herself. She isn't as helpless as you think Lenny.' When she'd gone I found her hair-band on the wall with some of her hair still caught in it. I meant to give it back to her the next day but forgot.

To make her point, and I think to annoy Mother, she gave me another present. It was a bright red t-shirt. Lettering on the front said 'Sydney Or Bust' above a picture of a kangaroo wearing sunglasses. She said 'If you don't make it that far you can always come and see me in Reading when I go to university.' I'd never been to Reading but I had seen it on the map and I knew it was a long way off, so I asked her if she could go to university here in the town. I wasn't sure if there was a university here, but it seemed like a nice idea. I could tell by her face that she didn't agree.

'Don't you get bored Lenny? A good lookin' bloke like you should get himself out there.'

'I've got plenty to keep me busy here.'

'God, I'd go mad if I had to stay here another month.' She must have seen my expression because she said more quietly, 'Sorry Lenny. Didn't mean…well you know.'

'It's okay. I know what you mean.' I didn't, but I was worried I had embarrassed her. Until then I had managed to forget that she would be leaving soon.

I couldn't wear the t-shirt she had given me so I placed it with her hair band into a tin and hid them in The Place. Mother had become so inquisitive that even the shed was no longer safe. I remembered the day when I had returned from school with a pornographic magazine that had been found by one of the other boys. I recalled how thoroughly I had hidden it and Mother's fury when she found it, and I put the trowel that she had given to me with the other things where they were invisible and safe from the rest of the world.

When the end of summer came, Mother fell ill and looking after her meant when Marianne went away I didn't get to say goodbye to her. She had promised to send me her address but it never came. Perhaps the letter was lost in the post, but I expect she was busy with her new life. I missed her and all through autumn and for a long time afterwards I watched for any sign of her, but she never came back. Sometimes, when I was working at the bottom of the garden out of sight of the house windows, I used the trowel she had given me and put on my t-shirt and hope that somehow they would bring her back. Then I would wrap them up and return them to The Place.

I often thought how nice it would've been to go and visit her but Mother needed me and I always knew that I would never go to Sydney, Reading or anywhere else so I tried to make myself forget her. And then, one day, I went down to the wall at the forgotten end of the garden, and it was gone: The Place and everything I had put in it had disappeared, replaced with the solid dirty wall made from the same stuff as the rest of the world. The things I had kept to remind me of Marianne and the letters that my father had kept safely hidden in his diaries until his death, had vanished. Marianne, Sandra and my father were all gone and with them all the signs of the worlds I had imagined. It was just me and Mother and the bricks and soil of where we lived.

Much later, in desperation, I tried to find the things I had lost by chiselling through the wall, but there was no sign of anything other than solid bricks. It had never occurred to me that one day The Place might disappear as quietly as it had arrived.

To my older eyes, the bottom of the garden seems

darker and smaller than it once was. Of course it's all mine now that Mother has gone. I still feel more comfortable down by the apple trees, out of sight of the windows, near the spot where Marianne kissed me. It was so long ago I have forgotten what it felt like.

I still tap the wall sometimes when I go past, just to be certain, and I still listen for Marianne's voice.

Adrian Sells

Thingummy Wotsit

'Can I take that tray now, luv?'

It's the slightly older nurse, the one who's a bit on the plump side. Her voice hauls me out of a light sleep, but one in which I've been dreaming again – strange dreams as usual. This time featuring what was he called? I remember now – Freddy, Freddy Allsop. Why I should be dreaming about Freddy Allsop I couldn't possibly say. I mean I haven't seen the bloke for seventy years or so. Not since school.

'Have you finished?' she continues.

'Yes, dear,' I say, although I've barely touched what's on my plate. Not because it's bad, I'm just not hungry.

She takes the tray and wheels away the little bed table, before bustling out of the room.

We were great rivals – Freddy Allsop and I. On the football pitch, in the classroom, for the lead role in "The Importance of Being Earnest". And then, of course, for the juiciest girl we both knew. Honours were pretty much divided between us, but I got the girl first. Then I gave her up for that lead role. Let Freddy have her – after all, I'd got there first.

You may be wondering what I mean about giving her up for that lead role and I'll explain. It was all about my dealing with God. Back then, I used to believe that actions had consequences, moral consequences. That everything fitted into some sort of general ethical framework and that good results were the reward for doing good things, or stopping doing bad things. That's why I was forever making deals with God along the lines of if I do such and such, will You make this or that happen for me. Although it was more often a case of my promising to stop doing the bad things, and mostly those bad things had something to do with sex, and usually the schoolboy's solitary sex habit. In this case I promised to give up what I was doing with wotsername if I could be Ernest.

It worked, or at least at the time I thought it worked. With the benefit of hindsight, I realise that it was just a matter of luck – like everything in life. Anyway I played the main part and Freddy got to be Algernon.

And that was pretty much the last time I saw him. The play marked the end of the academic year and our last term at school. By the time we left, war had started and I joined the army while I think he signed up with the navy. So why I should be dreaming of him now is pretty inexplicable.

It was the war that put paid to my making deals with God. It became apparent that somebody wasn't keeping his end of the bargain. Who lived and who died, who got injured and who promoted was all chance. Or that's the way I saw it then – a world ruled by randomness.

More recently I've started to play a different kind of game, and this time with what I think of as fate rather than God. It has no moral dimension. For example, I'll be sitting at my computer and decide to play a game of hearts and use the outcome of that as a guide to whether I'm likely to be successful at something else that I'm thinking about doing. Or I'll put the kettle on in my kitchen and then go about the business of gathering together my mug, the instant coffee and the sugar. If I am able to put two spoons of coffee and one of sugar into the mug, and return the jars to their proper places before the electric kettle boils and clicks off, then I've won and it means I will be blessed with a positive result in something else. It's my version of the Delphic oracle I suppose. Increasingly the answers I seek relate to how much longer I'm likely to live.

Another nurse comes into the room – it's the pretty Indian girl. She has a quick look at the old bloke in the opposite corner and satisfies herself that he's okay. As usual he's asleep. This is my second day here and we've yet to exchange a word because he's always spark out. There are tubes coming out of him all over the place and he doesn't seem to eat or go to the loo. A couple of times some staff have roused him to shift his position and I've had a look at him, but no conversation has occurred. Funnily enough he reminds me a bit of someone I used to know – only older of course.

Then the Indian nurse comes over to me. My God, she's so gorgeous. Tall for a girl from that subcontinent, quite light skinned, with high cheekbones you could cut yourself on and a mass of the most lustrous inky black hair you've ever seen.

'Everything all right, Mr Whitney?' she asks with clipped and very precise articulation. Her voice is as sexy as the rest of her.

'Fine, thank you. Although I'd love you to wheel back that table and pass me the notebook and pen from the cupboard down there,' I say, pointing to the bedside unit. I want her to stay a while. I also want her to bend down again and watch the tight uniform come under a bit of pressure in all the right places. I think she wears it tight deliberately: this girl knows she's got it.

Some people think that old codgers like me lose the urge. Although it may be true for some, it isn't for me. In many ways I often think life would be a great deal simpler if I had. The trouble is the urge is still there, but almost invariably without the remotest possibility of consummating it.

Take this girl, for instance. She's probably early twenties and I look at her through my eighty-eight-year-old eyes, but with a heart and a head that seem sixty years younger. I feel I ought to be able to chat her up as if I was still her age, charm her into bed. It's a huge disappointment to realise you're of absolutely no interest to women like this. Nor to women of thirty, forty, fifty or even sixty – and, frankly, I don't find seventy or eighty year-olds that attractive. Then you look in the mirror and have to turn away quickly, shocked by the wreck that stares back at you. If I was loaded like Hugh Hefner or that billionaire – the one who married Anna something or other – then I too could get lucky. But I'm not – I'm comfortably off as they say, but not rich. This definitely limits the options. I can still yearn and dream though. And flirt a little, always remembering to keep it the right side of dirty old man.

'So, was that your daughter who came to see you this morning?' she asks, bobbing up at my bedside with the notebook and pen in her hand.

'Yes…yes, my daughter, she did pop in,' I say, trying to remember her visit.

'She is a very beautiful woman.'

'Yes, but not quite as beautiful as you.' Oh God, I might as well be twirling a moustache and leering at her. However, she giggles cheerfully enough and seems to take it in good part.

'I have a son as well,' I say, changing tack. 'I think he may be coming in later.'

'That's nice,' she replies.

'Yes, he's a good chap…very witty and amusing. I said to him a few years ago, "I'm quite worried about Alzheimer's – if you ever see me going that way, make sure you tell me." And he said, "But Dad, we have."'

She smiles, but I'm not sure she gets the joke. Then I suddenly panic that I may have told it to her before.

'So what is it that you write in your book?'

'Oh, all sorts of things. It's a kind of journal I suppose. I used to write for a living and it's a habit I can't break.'

'What kind of books did you write?'

'I'm more of a journalist…a war correspondent for many years. Then I used to write features, profiles, that sort of thing, when I got too old to head off to the war zones.'

'That must have been a very interesting life,' she says, plumping up the pillows behind my head. 'Anything else you need at the moment?'

I can't think of anything. She smiles again and breezes out of the room.

She's right: it was an interesting life. Very much in the past tense. I'm not complaining, mind you. I stopped working full-time only ten years ago and kept my hand in with the occasional piece until I was eighty-five, which ain't bad.

Nowadays it is true that I write out of habit I suppose, although it was a little disingenuous of me to say that I keep some sort of journal. I do make notes of things that have happened, but I also write down things that I must do. I order it all in my little book; it's the way I keep on top of things. You see, the joke about Alzheimer's – like all good jokes – has an element of truth in it. The little grey cells are not what they were.

If I were younger or just more technically inclined I'd use one of those electronic wotsits. But I'm not, so down it all goes in longhand in my little book. And I think I'm coping – just. It is getting harder every day though.

I'm worried because my own father went this way a few years younger than I am now. Like me, he lived by himself and eventually my brothers and I decided it was just too dangerous for him to continue on his own. He might wander out and forget to lock the front door or forget to turn the gas off on the cooker. There were countless possible ways he might get himself into trouble. So we moved him into a nursing home. He put up only minor resistance. Once there and relieved of all the responsibilities for looking after himself, it was extraordinary how quickly his mind just gave up. Within days he simply seemed to have no memory any more, except for occasional bizarre fragments dredged up from the distant past. People commented on how relaxed and happy he was, and sure enough he always seemed to have a smile on his face. But he was a zombie, a void, who recognised nobody and knew nothing. It was fortunate, I think, that he died within three months of entering that nursing home. There was no point to him any more.

I'd asked for my notebook to keep that lovely nurse in the room a little longer and watch her stretching down beside my bed. But now something that she said makes me want to check it quite urgently. She mentioned that my daughter, Claire, had been to see me that morning. To be honest, it had slipped my mind and I want to recall the nature of our conversation. Anything important I write down. I'm sure she probably just made the sort of small talk that you do when you visit someone in hospital, but you never know.

I read my scribblings and it comes back to me. How could I have forgotten? She asked me whether I thought I could still cope on my own. I replied that of course I could, I'd just had a little accident – that might've happened to anyone. She said that she'd come back later with Simon, my son.

As I think about this I am frightened, more frightened than I've ever been. And I speak as someone who fought in the Second World War and was a journalist covering pretty much every war since then up until the

Falklands. Korea, Cyprus, Vietnam, Ireland, Indo-Pakistan, Nigeria, Angola and forever in the Middle East: I was there and others I can't remember. And I was very scared on many occasions, scared that I would die or be maimed. I was terrified when my daughter drank a whole bottle of medicine when she was six and nearly went into a coma. But nothing compares to this – a huge black hole of fear that completely engulfs me.

'Oh God,' I groan.

'Are you all right, mate?'

It's the old chap on the other side of the room, the fellow full of tubes. He's sitting up and looking at me. He reminds me of somebody, somebody I knew at school. I realise I'm crying, that tears are rolling down my cheeks.

'Do you want me to call for the nurse?'

I stare at him, shaking slightly and still weeping. Who is it he reminds me of? Then I remember. It's wotsisname, you know…thingummyjig.

'I'm fine,' I say eventually, clearing my throat. 'Just need a moment or two.'

'Are you sure?'

'Absolutely – just one of those things. Nothing to worry about.'

'Well, if you say so.'

He rolls on to his side and I hear no more from him. I decide to do the same and enjoy some sleep.

I wake to hear voices a little way from my bed. I realise one of them is my son's. I think I have been dreaming, but I can't remember what about. Simon is talking to my favourite nurse. He's flirting with her, and by the way she's standing in her tight uniform I can tell. It's her wotsitcalled…you know…body language. I can tell she's enjoying it. It's not surprising; he's very good-looking and only thirty-something. Product of my second marriage, you see. Claire, my daughter, is twenty years older.

Part of me is proud of my boy, as he effortlessly charms my Indian beauty; part of me is seething with anger. She's my nurse, not his. What is she doing laughing at his jokes like that, batting her giraffe eyelashes, arching her back a little, twiddling provocatively with the button on the front of her uniform just where the curve of her gorgeous breasts is at its fullest?

Hands off, I want to scream. Leave her for me. And now he's giving her something. Is it his card? He's scribbling on it. A home number? What else could it be? He holds her hand a moment as he passes it to her, longer than necessary. She's on one leg, the other curled behind it. She's squirming with pleasure at this contact. What would she do if I took her hand? Shiver probably.

I can't take any more of this and cough loudly. They look over, standing back from each other guiltily.

'Hi, Dad,' says Simon.

'Ah, Mr Whitney. You see your son has arrived,' she says, somewhat redundantly. 'I'll leave you together.'

Simon comes over and perches on the side of my bed. I notice his eyes following her out of the room.

'What a great girl,' he says.

'Hmm?'

'Shreya…the nurse. Come on, Dad, you must have noticed. She's a knockout. Lives up to her name: Shreya means beautiful in Hindi apparently.'

'I'll take your word for it,' I mutter grumpily.

'What's up? It's unlike you not to notice a pretty face.'

'I presume you came here to see me, not to chat up the hospital talent. Taking her out then are you?'

'Don't be silly. Although come to think of it, that's not a bad idea.'

'Are you denying that you gave her your number? I saw you just now.'

I realise I'm sounding angrier than I ought to.

'Steady on. Anybody'd think you were jealous or something.'

It's inconceivable of course to Simon that at my age I could be.

'Anyway,' he continues, 'I was giving her my contact details for professional reasons.'

'What? Is she thinking of a change of career?'

He laughs.

'No, no. It's just in case…you know…if the hospital needs to get hold of me. In an emergency…or something.'

'A likely story.' I manage a grin. 'I'm as right as rain in any case, just a couple of bruises.'

'And the cracked ribs and…'

'It's really not that serious. I'll be out of here in a day or so.'

'I like the spirit, Dad.'

We natter on now happily and my mood lightens. I know that I'm a silly old fool. Why shouldn't he chat up the nurse? Why shouldn't they see each other, come to that? In fact, I would be happy if they did. I almost manage to convince myself.

Then Claire arrives again, her brow furrowed, an aura of gloom clinging to her. She greets us both and we all exchange a few pleasantries before she suggests to Simon that they go and get a cup of tea. Subtlety was never Claire's strong point. I suppose I should be grateful that they're at least withdrawing to discuss me. In the last few years I've had to get used to people talking about me as if I'm not there.

I pick up my book and check the last few entries. I make some notes, including one that the nurse's name is Shreya. She may have told me before in which case I've forgotten. But now it's in my book.

It's not long before Simon and Claire return. They've brought a cup of tea for me. She still looks glum. He looks – I'm not really sure how to describe it – crestfallen, I suppose. I feel like I'm tiptoeing around the edge of a huge black hole again, but I smile cheerily and thank them for my tea.

After a few awkward moments, it's Simon who eventually raises the subject.

'You remember that jokey comment about Alzheimer's, Dad?'

'Of course I do,' I reply. 'I'm always telling people about it, how quick-witted you are. Still makes me laugh.'

They look at each other meaningfully.

'That's slightly the point, Dad. You do tell that story a lot. In fact, you tend to repeat yourself a great deal these days and we – that's Claire and I – we're just wondering about the serious side of that little anecdote …whether we need to warn you that you may be going in that direction.'

I feel myself being pushed closer to the edge of the vast dark chasm, but I remain cheery.

'I'm getting old that's all. I'm afraid we all repeat ourselves a little as we get on…'

'A lot,' chips in Claire. 'You repeat yourself a lot.'

'All right, a lot – if you insist. And you're right to keep an eye on things. And don't think I'm not grateful, but I'm fine at the moment.'

'Hardly fine,' says Claire. 'You're in hospital for Chrissake.'

'An accident – anybody can have an accident,' I protest.

'The point is, Dad,' says Simon. 'You remember

telling us about when you decided to do something about grandpa? You did it because you thought things had got to a point where he might be at risk. You worried that he might leave the gas on or his front door open.'

'Yes,' I say, truly terrified now, really teetering on the edge. 'But I was hit by a motorbike.'

'I know, I know – but it's a lapse of concentration and we're just a bit worried that it may be part of a general problem and that we ought to prepare for change.'

'Did I leave the front door open?'

'No, Dad, don't worry about that.'

I step back a little from the edge. I think I even sigh out loud.

'As I said, it was an accident. The wotsit chappy – you know the fellow on the bike – he was bound to have been going too fast.'

'Not what he says,' says Claire.

'Well, m'lud, he wouldn't admit it, would he? He'd lose his job, you know…'

'Couriering,' says Simon.

'Yes that's it – he was a courier.'

I feel triumphant, like a man who's proved his case. Simon shoots Claire a look as if to say that the old boy has a point. She glares back at him.

'Listen, we don't have to make any decisions about this right now, but perhaps you ought to start thinking about the future,' continues Simon eventually.

'What? You mean a home?'

'Well, actually, Claire was thinking that you could go and live with her and William. You know, they've got that nice annex and now the children are at uni it's more or less unused. It could be done up and you could live there.'

I should be touched by this offer. I know I should.

But, frankly living next door to my daughter and her prissy, pompous husband is no more appealing a prospect than being packed off to the nearest nursing home. Nevertheless, I manage a gracious smile.

'That's very kind of you, darling, but can we leave it there for the moment – as just a thought?'

'Fine,' she says, unable to keep a note of huffiness out of her voice. However, she promises to make some preparations, just in case. And we all agree to keep an eye on things, monitor my recovery and so on. I try to make a mental note to check whether I've already signed a power of attorney. I think there's been some talk of it, but I'm not sure whether it's gone any further than that.

When we've all kissed each other goodbye and my children have left me to my own devices again, I feel relieved. I reach for my book and quickly note developments, particularly this new suggestion that I might go and live with Claire and her husband. I don't really understand this extraordinary act of generosity. After all, we don't particularly get on – I don't think she's ever forgiven me for leaving her mother. There must be a hidden agenda. I'm sorry to sound so suspicious, but there must be. Perhaps they think they'll sell my house and get their hands on the proceeds. It's not nice to say it of my own flesh and blood, but this girl is definitely more of a Goneril than a…a wotsername – the nice one in Lear, you know.

I look back a page and read again my guilty secret. I regret now that I wrote it down. There really was no need: this is one thing that I'm not going to forget and the last thing I want anybody else discovering, particularly Claire or Simon. You see, I know I wasn't looking when that poor biker lad hit me. I was in a panic to get home, I was rushing and paying absolutely no attention because I only had one thing on my mind – whether or not I'd actually shut the front door when I'd left my house a couple of minutes earlier.

Now I know that I had.

I browse a few more pages, but can't find anything about the power of attorney business and eventually I put the book aside and have another little nap.

When I wake I am aware of having dreamt again, but have no idea about what. The other chap – the one with all the tubes in him – is propped up in bed now, but still apparently asleep. I can see his face quite clearly, however, and he definitely reminds me of someone.

The pretty nurse comes in and I enquire after his name. She wonders why.

'It's just that he looks like someone I used to know…someone called…oh thingummy,' I say. 'Something Allsop.'

'Not the same guy,' she says. 'His name is Mr Herring.'

I think she wears her uniform a size too small quite deliberately: the girl knows she's got it. She plumps my pillows and wonders if I enjoyed seeing my daughter and son earlier. I vaguely remember them coming in and the recollection fills me with an undefined sense of dread, but I look cheerful and say that it was lovely. I tell her how charming and bright my son is and how quick-witted, and I recount a little illustration of this from a while back when he and I exchanged some banter about Alzheimer's. She smiles benignly but doesn't laugh. I wonder if she gets the joke.

Angela Sherlock

Set Dance

Dance at home

'I was thinking,' said Willie, as he stood at the sink, 'of going over to Leenane for the fair.' He swirled water over the plates and laid them out on the wooden draining board. His brother said nothing. 'It is next Tuesday,' he went on, 'so that would mean…' Christy interrupted him. 'I know when it is. And since we are not in present need of a ram, why are you going?' Willie thought a moment before he turned round to face into the room.

His brother still sat at the table, the paper spread across the oil cloth, and he was glaring up at Willie. The October evening had darkened the windows and Christy read by the light of an oil lamp at his elbow. In the grate, peat glowed and flickered, sending shadows around the walls. 'Just to see some of the fellas,' said Willie, 'and maybe…' He paused. 'There's a dance in the evening. I was, er, I was thinking of maybe looking in there.' Christy snorted and rustled the paper.

'So, it's to the dance you are going?' His voice rose in scorn. 'And who was it you were thinking of dancing with? I do not imagine there will be any women your age looking for partners.' Willie was startled by the anger in his brother's voice and he hunched his shoulders defensively.

'It is only for a bit of craic, Christy. Sure it's not often that we get away and I thought…'

'What did you think? That you'd find some girl to marry? Another Nora Geraghty? Someone daft enough to marry a fifty year old Mayo farmer – who is going bald?' He smacked his hand down on the paper. 'And how were you thinking of getting to Leenane? And back afterwards, with drink taken, I suppose?' Willie folded his arms across his chest and fixed his eyes on Christy's receding hairline.

'John-Joe has two rams he is taking and I will ride with him. I had thought, Christy, that you might like to come too, but…' He did not allow the smile to reach his lips as he turned to the sink. The reflection that looked back at him from the darkened window reassured him that he need not worry about his age, or his hair. He heard Christy's chair scrape over the flags as he stood.

'I will see about the butter,' he announced as he crossed through to their dairy room. Willie could hear the bad tempered clatter of churns and pans as he wiped the dishes and returned them to the dresser. Nora Geraghty. Ah now, there was an opportunity missed. A lovely young woman, indeed. And didn't she marry that O'Reilly fella, back from the States with money in his pocket. He's not much younger than me, Willie told himself, and I would say we are about the same height. Though she's taller, that's true. And on his way out to the cowshed Willie was painting pictures of the pretty women he would meet at Leenane and how he would sweep one off in his arms and bring her back to the farm.

The bedroom was a problem, though, he had to admit. Christy was the firstborn and so had moved into their parents' bedroom with the big double bed that stood brave in the middle of the room. The boys had been conceived and born in that bed, and both their parents had died in it. Shouldn't the handsome room be relinquished to him and his bride, even though he was the younger? When he went up to his own room that night, Willie felt aggrieved at the smallness of it and the narrowness of his bed. But he had pleasant dreams and awoke good humoured enough to cajole Christy into coming with him and John-Joe the next week. And, truth to tell, there was not much persuading needed.

A rain storm battered the brothers into wakefulness the day of the fair and both felt glum as they moved around the dark kitchen. They took tea only, for John-Joe was coming up to collect them. 'We'll get away early and ye can eat at Leenane,' he had assured them. Christy piled blocks of the slow burning stone peat onto the embers, so that they would not come home in the night to a cold house. While he was counting out their money from the rusty box that was kept under the stair, Willie stood at the door, on the watch for John-Joe. They were to go out down the boreen and wait for him at the lower gate but the rain was flying everywhere and they would not stand out in it longer than need be.

'Sure, the only thing that Mayo has plenty of is bad weather,' he said, looking mournfully out into the wet darkness.

'Ah, well,' said Christy, coming to stand beside him. 'Isn't it a good thing, then, that we are off to Galway for the day?' And they grinned at each other.

Advance and retire

Although the brothers were not trading the day was full of interest for them. The black faced rams of Leenane were famous and Willie and Christy prodded and examined and questioned along with the best of them. They agreed privately that John-Joe could have got a better price but to his face congratulated him on his business acumen. They watched with delight as one pair of rams started to bang their skulls together, the smaller driving the bigger beast into the corner of the pen then attacking with his horns and drawing blood. 'Whose are they?' Christy asked his neighbour, but no one seemed to know the owner and the circle of men did not trouble themselves to intervene.

'Why don't you stop them?' Willie turned to see a

small woman beside John-Joe. 'Why don't you stop them? Sure, they'll kill each other.' John-Joe looked down upon her indulgently. 'Ah, missus, and why would we? They'd need to be parted and where are they to be put? The owner would think we were stealin' them.' She shook her head, and Willie was delighted at the way her hair danced and glinted. She felt him looking at her and turned to him, a frown creasing her forehead and her lips parted to speak. He looked away quickly to find Christy smiling at him.

'Not that one, I think, boy,' he whispered. 'That's Kate Calvey and she must be at least twenty years younger than you.'

'Then she's twenty three years younger than yourself,' Willie retorted, anger making his voice carry so that Kate heard and looked hard at him. Just then, the owner of the fighting rams arrived and strode through the crowd. He grabbed the aggressor by his haunches and pulled the ram away.

'Will we go in for a pint now?' said John-Joe and the three of them pushed their way into the crowded bar. Christy insisted that he should pay and while he was struggling up to the counter, Willie interrogated John-Joe.

'Is she married, that Kate Calvey? And where is she from? And do you know her people?' His eagerness amused John-Joe but, although he set himself up as an authority on everything, he knew nothing of the woman and was obliged to avoid giving straight answers. Christy shoved his way back to them with three pints held high, jammed precariously against each other. The fair had enticed farmers from many miles around and the room was full of their smell and their voices. Willie tried to draw back from his neighbour, his eyes sliding away from the ugly red swelling that protruded through his hair. As he looked around, it seemed to him that many of these men were disfigured. There were blemishes on faces, hunched backs, mutilated hands. He wondered if perhaps he did not look quite handsome in comparison. The trio drank several pints then bundled down the road for a meal of stew, piled high with potatoes. There was not a woman in the place; men, many of them ancient and solitary, were dotted down the long tables. He sat opposite a silent old fellow, a mass of white hair sprouting from his head and his cheeks and his chin. When Willie went up to pay he saw the old man was bent over his wad of money, secretively counting out the notes, dipping his head up and down to check that no one was watching.

The daylight was beginning to fade when they stepped out into the street. Willie stopped to admire two pups that were lined up for sale. He bent down to examine them and their mother came over to inspect him. When Willie put out his hand to stroke her, the bitch cringed and her owner put out his boot to shove her away. As they went off down the street, Christy said, 'I'd not trust that one. Did you see the fear in that bitch? And if I'm not mistaken that's one of Henry McNally's boys. A bad lot.'

Christy and John-Joe decided that another drink was in order before going to take a look in at the dancing, but Willie felt the need of a walk, 'to settle me stomich'. He wandered down the road and stood looking into the darkening waters of the harbour. Away to the west, where the fjord opened out into the Atlantic, there was still some light hanging above the horizon. He looked up at the great shoulders of mountain that crowded against the sky and a fit of melancholy seized him. Had he really thought there would be some woman here who would like the look of him? All those dances he had gone to when he was a young man tumbled into his memory to taunt him. He had set out with such high hopes. The shoes polished, the shirt ironed and crackling with starch and his big hands scrubbed to a painful redness. There was always that pause outside the dance hall door, when he would gather himself in tight as the music rolled out to greet him. Then it was quickly over to the bar, head up and staring straight ahead, to join the other lads. They stood in a cloud of tobacco smoke and held on fiercely to their pints while reviewing the groups of young women who stood around on the other side of the hall.

The first act of bravery was to select one and ask her for a dance. Willie, of course, had started by choosing the beauties but over the years he contented himself with the girls who were last to be asked out onto the floor. He was a good dancer, upright and lively, his feet making the intricate patterns and cheerful stamps on the boards that the music demanded. And he loved the feel of a woman in his arms as couples swung across the set. But it was afterwards that he failed. When the music was over and the dancers stood panting and laughing, he had no words to say. Nothing would come into his head, not the weather or the crops or any questions to draw her out. Willie would mumble his thanks and retreat to the bar, his disappointed partner returning to her friends. He had watched in agony as they put their heads together and, he felt sure, judged and found him wanting. Christy, too, he imagined, had suffered in much the same way but it was never spoken of. Over the years, Willie lost all hope and with his hopes went his dancing.

He turned back to the lights of the village and marched up the road. If Christy and John-Joe were for going home, then he would not be at all sorry. But when he shouldered his way into the dance hall they were in the thick of it and he knew he would have to stay. The thought of another pint made his gorge rise. The brothers had developed abstemious habits simply because the farm lay so far from the Bridgeport road that to go out for a night's drinking was not practicable. A bottle of whisky was kept on the dresser, its shoulders dusty because visitors were so few. Sometimes a tinker would trade them some poteen for a night's lodging, but the flask of clear, fiery liquid could sit for years untouched.

'Do you not dance, then?' Her voice made him turn in surprise. She had put her hair up since the afternoon and was tapping her foot in time to the music.

'I do so,' he blurted out, then was instantly seized with the fear that he would have lost all his skill. 'At least, I…I used.'

'Well then, perhaps you should ask me…' Kate Calvey tipped her head to one side and Willie's heart seemed to tilt within him at the same angle. Without a word, he held out his arms and the pair moved out onto the dance floor.

Show the lady

As the music got into his feet, Willie forgot to feel self-conscious. He swung back and forth, holding her hand, or her elbow, or her waist, as the dance demanded. She bobbed up and down, opposite, beside him, across the set, and, to his heart's joy, all the movements lived again in his feet. Willie did not know that he was smiling. When the dance ended he came to a standstill, panting and laughing. That Kate Calvey had no more words than he did was an added delight. He put his hand upon her elbow and guided her from the floor.

'Would ye like a drink?' he asked, and hurried off to

the bar. But there was a crowd before him and by the time he got back, Kate was gone. He stood with her glass of cordial in his hand and Willie O'Brien felt like a fool.

'Sure, she's only off with John-Joe.' Christy was beside him, waving across the dance floor to where little Kate was linking arms with John-Joe, his mighty belly waggling between them in a friendly way. Willie tapped his foot and looked unconcerned and did not know what to do with her glass. When the set ended and she came from the floor, Kate threw him a grateful glance as she gulped the liquid down. Her hair was damp with sweat and he looked with longing at the sheen of it on her upper lip.

The musicians took a break then, which left the trio of men with only conversation to entertain her. John-Joe launched into the story of selling his rams and the journey back they would have on the narrow, dark road to Bridgeport.

'Oh, ye are from Bridgeport then?' she asked Willie, but Christy replied for him.

'Near enough, but out beyond the crossroads, on the road to Killeen then a ways up into the hills.' He hurried on. 'A good little farm we have, with some cattle and some sheep. We keep some poultry and also the sow, but a woman is needed to turn that into a profitable enterprise, with all the rest we have to do.' Kate ignored this and asked,

'And who is minding it for you this day?' which sent Christy off into a tirade against young Tommy Shelton and the mess he would have made of the work. Willie shifted from foot to foot but was finally obliged to struggle through the mass of bodies and go out the back of the hall to relieve himself. The morning's rainclouds had been battered away by the wind coming in off the sea and he stood to look up at the stars in the black sky. When he went back in, Kate was gone, danced off first by Christy and then John-Joe, and didn't Christy get another dance in before they lost her. His last sight of her was being spun across the set by the McNally boy.

Chain

Their journey home was perilous, John-Joe awash with stout and in constant danger of tipping them off the road. In the end, Willie took the reins and let the other two sag into sleep. He had some difficulty getting them into the house and had to abandon the pair so that he could get the horse stabled and check that young Shelton had carried out all his tasks. When he went back into the kitchen he was relieved to find that John-Joe was stretched out on the settle, a blanket draped crookedly across him, and Christy seemed to have made it up the stairs.

Willie lay down in his bed and mocked himself for the hopes of the morning. A fifty year old farmer, and yes, maybe his hair was thinning a bit, going off to the dance and thinking he could bring back a bride. He could not settle to sleep, remembering the feel of the woman in his arms and the tickle of her hair against his face. He could not bring to mind the colour of her eyes, only that they were bright and full of laughter. What age would she be? And how did Christy know of her? So long since a woman had been in this house. He thought of his mother, a short, round woman who had always seemed old to him. But she had died younger than he was now. Strange to think of that. The yard had been a swirl of poultry in her day and it seemed to Willie that she had always hummed and sung at her work. How long since anyone had sung in this house? He sank into melancholy and at last drifted off into a miserable sleep.

Rain battering at the windows woke him to a grey day that matched his mood. Wrapped in self pity he went down to rake up the fire and was surprised to find John-Joe seated at the table with a plate of bacon and potatoes.

A cheerful 'Ah, young Willie,' greeted him, and Christy turned from the range to say if he wanted eggs he'd to fetch them himself because young Shelton hadn't bothered to collect them yesterday.

'Well, that was a grand day out,' John-Joe announced. 'How's the head, Willie? A lie-in usually does the business and, if not, a fry up is a great cure.'

'Some of us got more sleep than others on the way home,' Willie said shortly, and ignored the grins that his sourness produced. When John-Joe had got his traps together and was ready to set off towards Bridgeport, the brothers walked out with him to close the gates and see him on his way. As he set off he called back over his shoulder,

'Great changes coming, boys. I don't suppose I'll be let sleep in yon kitchen the next time.' As they walked back up the boreen, sacks pulled over their heads to keep the rain off, Willie puzzled over the comment.

'Why would he not be?' he shouted through the downpour, but Christy was hunched against the rain and did not hear him. They shook off the wet in the porch and left the sacks on a hook to drip.

'How did Tommy fare yesterday?' Christy asked. 'Apart from the eggs. Were the beasts in and all well? I was in no state to check after lugging that great galoot to his bed. He's a heavy man and a deal taller than meself…' Willie cut across him.

'What did he mean about great changes?' A dreadful thought came to him. 'He did not…he is not…yesterday, with Kate Calvey…?' Christy frowned at him and when he understood burst into a great shout of laughter.

'John-Joe and that wee girl,' he spluttered. 'Now, that would be something. No, sure, it's her coming here he meant and then he'll not be let sleep the night when he has some drink taken.' Willie's jaw dropped and he stared across the room at Christy. At first he could not summon the words. Kate coming here. There was no sense in it. Unless…

'Why?' he croaked, his throat dry and constricting on the word. 'Why?'

'Why what?' Christy said, and his chin came up as anger began to glint in his eyes. He said no more and folded his arms across his chest. They stood and looked at each other and for some minutes nothing was said. 'Well? What is it that you are asking?' Willie thought then that it was all lost and so nothing he said could matter.

'You have come to some arrangement, is it? You…and Kate Calvey?' He thought his voice sounded very thin in the silence of the kitchen. Christy glared across at him.

'We have, indeed, come to some arrangement. And as the head of the house amn't I let make decisions…' Then his face cleared. 'Ah, now and weren't you off out the back when it was settled.' He clapped his hands together. 'And I did not tell ye on the road home, now I think of it.' Willie steadied himself, holding on to the back of the chair, as he waited for the words to come. 'Her brother is married six months and the wife doesn't want Kate in the house. You know, two women in the same kitchen.' Christy paused as a thought struck him. 'Mind, two men don't seem to have any trouble with that, for don't you and me…? Anyway, how it is, Kate is looking for a situation and I told her we were in need of a housekeeper and to look after the hens and all, and I am to fetch her next week.'

Swing

Willie heard the trap and retreated to the door of the dairy. He saw Kate wrinkle her nose as she stepped into the kitchen and he sniffed the air to see what had offended her. Onions? Peat? Or maybe it was the dogs. Christy called him from the yard and Willie was obliged to reveal himself.

'Well, Mr O'Brien,' she said, holding out her hand and he had to come and shake it and mumble a response. Then,

'My brother wants me, I think,' he said and hurried outside.

'She's brought a lot with her,' Christy complained, as they heaved the trunk down. 'Is it all frocks, or what? Sure, we haven't as many clothes as this between the pair of us.'

'No, Mr O'Brien,' Kate called from the door. 'It's a lot of books too, and they do weigh heavy.' Christy reddened but his embarrassment was masked by the effort of carrying the trunk in. Kate thanked them.

'But what am I to call ye? You cannot both be Mr O'Brien.' Christy said what about their names and asked Willie to show Kate her room while he saw to the horse. Willie went up the stairs before her, worrying which part of his anatomy was level with her eyes. The boards creaked as he led her down the passage and the door creaked as he opened it. Kate laughed and said she'd not be able to creep about at night without getting caught, then, and he stood back to let her see in.

It was a narrow room, the bed down one side and a

dresser below the window. Three hooks were embedded in the wall and a wonky little stool sat just inside the door. He realised it was even smaller than his own but Kate shook herself and said it was grand. Willie thought from the tone of her voice that perhaps it was not, and tried to make amends.

'We, er, we can put up some shelves for you…for the books, you know…and, er, perhaps somewhere for…for clothes…' He left her to get settled and went back down to heave the trunk across to the bottom of the stairs. Since it would not fit in her room, Kate was obliged to make trips up and down with armfuls of garments and books, and Willie took himself off to the top field after the first terrifying glimpse of a bundle of stays and chemises.

The afternoon was awkward and the evening promised to be worse. Christy and Willie met in the yard before the light fell, worrying about what to do next.

'Will she eat some of that stew, d'you think? She'll not have had time to cook, yet, and…' Christy shrugged his shoulders, grimacing his ignorance of what to do next.

'Do housekeepers sit wi' ye in the evenin'?' he asked. 'Do they need entertainin' or what?' Willie paled at the thought, having no notion of how one entertained a woman beyond bobbing around a dance floor with her.

But Kate Calvey sorted them out. The meal was in progress by the time they went in and all she asked about was the breakfast and the poultry for the morning. She left the brothers at the table while she moved between the kitchen, the dairy and her room. The two ate in their usual silence, uncomfortably aware of her brisk movements and the creak of the boards overhead when she went upstairs. Willie felt awkward about leaving the dishes on the table but, 'Pish!' Christy whispered to him, 'Isn't that what we're paying her for?' This left them with little occupation for the evening and they sat stiffly on either side of the fire with sections of the Gazette opened, but largely unread.

'What happens about washing?' Willie whispered across to his brother and they stared at each other in horror. Their evening ablutions were performed at the kitchen sink, the morning wash usually at the pump in the yard, and the tin bath was brought in on Saturdays. They were still contemplating this difficulty when Kate came back down.

'Have ye's a jug and basin,' she asked, 'to take up the stairs to my room?' The brothers stared at her, then, when he understood, Christy shook himself and got up.

'I think Mama had one. I don't know where it's got to…' but Willie was before him.

'Bottom of the larder,' he said, 'in the dairy.' and hurried out to get it for her. Kate went to put a pot of water on the range but Christy carried it over for her.

'A bit heavy,' he muttered then did not know where to put himself, so he stood on the hearth and looked at his boots until Willie came back in.

'There's a wee crack in the ewer,' said Willie, 'but it should do until we get into Bridgeport and buy ye another.' Kate looked at his dusty offerings but only smiled across at the men.

'And a towel?' she asked, which caused another difficulty. No clean towel was to be found in the kitchen or the dairy but Willie had a thought.

'The press in your room, Christy,' he said. 'Mama had lots of things up there.' So all three trooped up to look, Christy first, carrying the lamp.

'Well, now, this is a grand room,' Kate said, which

embarrassed Christy, for the blankets were thrown back, exposing a grubby sheet. A pair of long johns hung over the bed rail, and a slightly rank smell was detectable. The press was a vast mahogany piece, grimy with dust, which took up most of one wall. The brothers had raided its contents for what they needed downstairs and had not looked inside it for many years. They stood to watch as Kate went through the shelves until she turned and said,

'Downstairs with ye both. I'll help meself and tell ye's what I've taken. Oh, and if that water's boiled one of you might fill the jug and put it up in my room.' They turned away quickly, Willie diving out first and galloping down the stairs to obey her. He had, then, to struggle back up with the hot jug, Christy coming behind him with the basin. There was nowhere to put it down in her room except upon the floor, the stool having lurched alarmingly when Willie planted the jug on it.

It was becoming obvious to them that having a woman in the house might not be all plain sailing. The brothers went early to bed that night. It seemed the simplest thing to do.

Round the house and mind the dresser

It took Kate Calvey less than three weeks to accomplish the transfer to the big bedroom. Publicly, Christy pretended not to mind. After all, it was reasonable with all the bits she had, and now she could also use it as her sitting room and leave the brothers the kitchen for the evenings. Privately, his resentment simmered and Willie feared that he would demand an exchange of their rooms, since he was the older. Kate, however, set about soothing Christy. She always referred questions of management to him and listened respectfully to his advice. Willie began to notice extra rashers creeping onto

Christy's plate. Kate was all eager attention when he came back from the market in Bridgeport, laughing at his tales and praising his skills.

A harsh winter set in and the work out of doors was punishing. The sky seemed always to be heavy with grey clouds and frost lay on the ground all day. Ice formed on the insides of the windows upstairs and when all the heat was gone from the stone water bottle Willie woke up shivering. He had taken to wearing one of his father's old nightcaps and he tugged it down over his ears, which were nearly numb with the cold. Should he go down and get a coat to put over him? The weight would produce some heat but the thought of stepping out into the cold deterred him. He was burrowing deeper under the blankets, tucking his hands between his knees, when he heard a door creaking open, followed by the groan of floorboards. Now, if Christy was going down for a coat maybe he would fetch one up for Willie. He was about to call out when he heard another bedroom door shut. No one had gone downstairs.

Willie lay awake for most of that night, rigid with anger and sorrow. The tension did not leave him until the sky was beginning to lighten.

Nothing was said the next morning but he was sure Christy was unusually cheerful. He waited for news of the wedding but it did not come. Each night he would try to stay awake, tormenting himself with every creak that the old house gave out as it shifted under the burden of the cold. In the days he took to watching and listening, but Kate and Christy seemed to go on much as before. Never talkative, he now withdrew into silence, responding only in grunts, and Christy took a rise out of him for it.

'Could youse not get out more than one syllable?' he asked. 'Surely to God, you could keep a civil tongue in your head now there's a lady in the house.' They were out in the yard, working on the pump which was beginning to seize up in the cold. Willie threw down his wrench and stood up square to his brother, his fists bunched.

'I do not need you, nor your damned lady, to be telling me how to behave.' He stood, red in the face, eyes hard, but Christy only looked at him in surprise. Kate saw, though. She was watching through the kitchen window and was at the door in a trice.

'Willie,' she called. 'Would you ever do something for me? I'm wanting to wash the curtains in the parlour and I cannot get them down on my own. If you could oblige me, by standing on a chair, and perhaps we could do it together...'

It wasn't until he was lying in bed that night that he remembered his mother had never washed curtains in December. For how would you dry them? But the thought was lost as his door creaked open and Kate Calvey came into his bed in her nightgown.

Slide and home

'It's a girl,' Adie Lafferty said. The quay was golden with sunlight and the islands in the bay were dancing in the heat haze. Adie had already toured the town with the news, the spreading of which was causing her to take a deal more exercise than usual. She fanned herself and wished a lady could dispense with stays in this heat. 'It came in the afternoon and was a long time about it, apparently.'

'Did they have a midwife, or what?' asked Mrs Collins. 'And how is Kate Calvey?' She looked over her shoulder then dipped her head closer to Adie. It wouldn't do to be seen gossiping but the whole town was interested in this news. Why, even the Marquis might wish to know of it. She thought she would just look in on his housekeeper before she walked home.

'Didn't Nora O'Reilly go up to do the birthing. She has a midwife for her own deliveries but there's not many in these parts can afford it. And wasn't that very Christian of her, especially,' here Adie's voice dropped to a whisper, 'considering the situation up there.' Her listener nodded, tightening her lips in disapproval.

'Is there any, er, resemblance…um, do they know…?' she asked.

'Not yet,' said Adie, with some satisfaction. 'Maybe time will tell. But the brothers aren't saying.' She paused to fan herself, loosening the top button of her blouse and wiping the sweat from her neck. 'Sure, wouldn't this heat kill yer?' She went on. 'I did ask Nora. I thought Kate Calvey might have said something, called out for one of them, you know? But that one considers herself too much the lady to be telling an'thing.' She shifted from foot to foot. 'Oh, my feet,' she grumbled. 'I'd best be off now while I can still walk. I have a few others to see yet.' Adie began to move away but turned back for a last word. 'Let's be looking out at church. Father Tiernan was up to the farm as soon as she was showing and the three of them have been coming to Mass bold as brass ever since. There's bound to be a baptism and, you never know, there might yet be a wedding in it.'

Paddy Nolan greeted Adie as she crossed the square and she was glad of the excuse to stop and catch her breath.

'Mrs Lafferty, do you not recognize this fella here?' indicating his son, Patrick. 'Back from England to keep his old dad company. And, yes,' he said, 'we've heard the news. Did you have a hand in that arrangement out at Killeen? For, if so, meself and the boy would be grateful to benefit from yer expertise.' He turned to Patrick. 'Wouldn't a housekeeper like that Kate Calvey just suit the pair of us?' he said, and the laugh he gave, as Adie confided to Dermot that evening, 'was very coarse. A nasty leer on his face, too. I will not be speaking with him again in a hurry.' Dermot only said,

'Yes, my dear,' and kept his eyes fixed on his paper.

Tim Collins shocked his wife by failing to find the event shocking.

'Didn't people manage their own affairs fine before the priests got into everything? There's lots of places in the world where it happens and it seems to me that how the O'Briens and Kate Calvey manage together is nobody's business but their own.' She accused him of being a heathen but Tim quite liked that notion and refused to take offense.

*

Willie and Christy weathered all the gossip. It was harder for Kate, and Bridgeport never did let the matter quite lie. But she brazened it out, taking her daughter to church every Sunday and always stopping to talk with old Father Tiernan. Going home for breakfast, Philomena would dance up the boreen ahead of the trio.

'Mind out for the mud on your Sunday dress,' Kate would call after her, but when the dogs dashed out to greet them the warning was forgotten.

'It'll wash,' said Christy, and 'It's no harm,' said Willie, and they smiled down upon their daughter.

Emma Martin

Victor

The concrete wall at the front of the clinic was low enough for Victor to sit on, but he always made a point of standing. His pamphlets, blotched through repeated photocopying, were in his carryall at his feet. His parka was zipped tight under his chin. In his hand was a placard showing a baby in utero, sun-faded orange, floating in its amniotic sea above the words 'Abortion Kills Unborn Children'.

He peered at the sky. Dense grey clouds scudded northwards, as if in a film running in fast motion. A car turned past him into the car park, two young women in the front seat. As they slowed over a speed hump, one wound down her window.

'Your mother should have aborted you, ya loser!'

Victor nodded his head slightly; almost a bow. He'd heard everything now: God squad, loony…and worse. It used to amaze him, the things people accused him of – of ramming his opinion down their throats – when the truth was it was they who attacked him, shouting, swearing, threatening. He had never done anything more than stand as witness while each day, today, in the building behind him, a woman was being led into a room, was removing her clothes, slipping her arms into a hospital gown, climbing onto a narrow table and lying, feet together, letting her knees fall open, while the doctor scrubbed his hands and told her there was nothing to worry about.

Sometimes, not often, people tooted and waved at Victor. Occasionally someone asked for one of his pamphlets. Once a white-haired Maori lady had placed a frail hand on his forearm and thanked him. But most people just ignored him: the commuters, the students, the hospital visitors, the parents with pushchairs. The doctors. The nurses.

Which have eyes, and see not; which have ears, and

hear not.

A heavily pregnant woman was passing, half jogging to keep pace with a blonde-haired child on a scooter. Her eyes avoided Victor's. He used to assume a kind of solidarity with pregnant women. After all, they knew the sanctity of life, accepted their role in bearing it. He had expected – he didn't know what – an acknowledgement, he supposed, that they were on the same side. But this never came. He found himself thinking about Maureen when she was pregnant with Lauren. She'd barely tolerated him touching her – at the time he'd put it down to anxiety after the miscarriages – but once she had allowed him to lay his hand on the hard mound of her belly and feel its secret undulations. He remembered her eyes watching him, cool and distant, her hair, which would fall out in clumps after Lauren was born and never properly grow back again, still thick and brown.

Victor rested his placard against the wall and poured tea from his thermos into a stained plastic cup. Overloaded buses queued to pick up more passengers. At the bus shelter, a gaggle of schoolboys in grey shorts and knee socks scuffled and barged and punched each other's biceps. One of them staggered backwards into a girl who was leaning against the shelter. She wrapped her arms around herself and stepped out of the way. She was wearing a dress with no coat; she must be cold. She had a ring in her nose. So many of the young ones these days had them. Victor could not comprehend why a girl – a perfectly nice looking young girl – would do this to herself. He'd never given Lauren permission even to have her ears pierced. Not that it made any difference; when she was thirteen she did it anyway. Victor remembered her earlobes red and swollen, weeping, and the faint smell of Dettol that followed her for weeks.

He finished his tea, wiped out the inside of the cup

with a handkerchief, clicked the cup back onto the thermos, and nested the thermos into its designated compartment in his carryall.

The traffic was starting to thin. Victor picked up his placard and watched a digger on the demolition site across the road. It drove improbably up a pile of rubble next to a half-flattened building, raised its arm in the air and repeatedly rammed the building's injured wall. As the concrete crumbled, whole rooms were exposed: what must have been a bathroom, a bedroom, a kitchen still with its shelves and cupboards, a picture hanging over the sink, curtains at the windows. Dust swirled, and flurries of grit blew into Victor's face. He squeezed his eyes closed.

'Excuse me,' said a voice. Victor turned. It was the girl with the nose ring.

'Yes?' he said.

It was not in her nostril, which would have been bad enough, but through the septum. It made him feel sick.

'I don't really know how to ask this.' She hesitated. 'I was wondering if…'

'If what?'

'I'm in trouble,' she said.

The racing clouds seemed to pause. Victor felt suddenly clear headed. For he had imagined this moment; imagined a girl, perhaps not exactly like this one, with her wan face and freckled arms – but not so very different either.

'You mean… You're…?'

The girl nodded.

Victor placed his hand awkwardly on her shoulder. She was skinny. Really quite fragile. She had a peculiar smell: thick, spicy, like the sachets of potpourri Maureen kept in the drawers in Lauren's old room.

'The thing is, my boyfriend doesn't want to know,' the girl said.

'Ah.'

'I don't know what to do.'

Her name was Soraya. She was eighteen. Victor offered to buy her a cup of tea and was pleased and a little alarmed when she accepted. They walked together to a cold, glass-fronted café in a cluster of shabby-looking shops, and sat at a corner table on moulded plastic chairs. She asked in a small voice if she could please have a soy latte. Victor ordered a cheese scone which came with a hard little knob of butter, and a custard square for Soraya. As she talked she picked at the pastry, and squidged her finger into the congealed filling.

Her boyfriend was the drummer in a band; they lived in a warehouse that was also the band's practice space. According to the boyfriend, the baby wasn't a person yet, not till it was much bigger. It was just a few cells. If she sorted it out soon, it would just be like a heavy period; he knew all about it.

Victor could feel his heart pounding, but kept his voice carefully level.

'How far along are you?'

'I don't know. I mean, not very...maybe a few weeks?'

Victor lifted the placard from its position propped against the table leg. The baby's head was haloed by white light. Its skin was translucent.

'This is eight weeks after conception. Only eight weeks – and look at it. Its heart is beating. It's got ten fingers, ten toes. Fingernails, even. Its fingerprints are already forming.'

'No,' said Soraya, her eyes widening.

'You know, by the time it's ten weeks old, it can suck its thumb.'

He paused. Soraya was biting her lip, and didn't reply. Victor took a sip of his tea, which had a soapy taste. He watched a woman with long, greasy hair tying an Alsatian to a lamp post outside the window.

'Do you believe in fate?' said Soraya suddenly.

'I'm not sure what you mean,' said Victor.

'Just that, well, maybe this baby wasn't meant to be.'

'And who do you think decides if the baby is "meant to be," as you put it?'

Soraya looked at Victor blankly. She shrugged.

'It doesn't sound like it's much use then, does it, this idea of fate of yours?' he said.

'I guess I'm just trying to figure out, you know, what I should do,' said Soraya. 'I mean, I don't know. I really don't know.' Victor noticed her hands were shaking. When she set down her coffee cup it jangled against the saucer. He felt a rush of sympathy for her.

'It's going to be okay,' he said.

'I just want to make it all go away.'

'I know you do.'

It turned out Soraya's problem was not just moral but practical. The boyfriend was threatening to kick her out of the warehouse if she didn't have an abortion.

'Isn't there at least a chance that he'll marry you?'

'Marry me?' Soraya's serious expression vanished for a moment, and she seemed to be stifling a laugh. 'You've got to be kidding.'

'I know you're still young, but things like this can be a blessing in disguise. Can make you grow up fast. It might be just what he needs.'

'Trust me, he's not going to marry me.'

'Well in that case,' said Victor, 'have you thought about adoption? There are people out there, good families, who are desperate for babies. Who would look after your baby. Love it.'

'I don't know if I could,' she said. 'Give it away.'

She placed her hand on the waistline of her dress.

'You need to think about what's best for the baby.'

'Yes, but –'

'The baby, Soraya.'

His words sounded sharper than he intended. She looked up at him, and he was struck once again by how tiny she was.

'But where would I go?'

Victor remembered a cousin he had grown up with, back in Rangiora, who left school in Form Five and went away to be a housekeeper for a family in Christchurch. He supposed they didn't do that now. She was different when she returned, that cousin. He had a feeling there'd been more trouble with her afterwards.

'Surely you've got someone? Family? A girlfriend you could stay with?'

Soraya shook her head. She'd moved here to be with her boyfriend; her friends were really his friends. Her parents were up north, in Whakatane. It seemed she didn't get on with them.

'Haven't you told them?' said Victor.

'I can't,' she said. 'They're not like you. Kind like you.' Her eyes flicked from the table top to Victor's face, then quickly down again. 'Do you have children?'

'A daughter.'

'How old is she?'

'A few years older than you.'

'What's she like?'

Victor hadn't seen Lauren for over a year. He suspected she visited Maureen when he wasn't home.

'She's…' He paused. 'She used to be a lovely girl.' He had a sudden, vivid memory of Lauren aged six, crouching on the grass in her Womble pyjamas, watching him nail chicken wire to the frame of her rabbit hutch. That hutch, rotted beyond recognition, was still somewhere down the damp end of the section, buried in wandering jew.

'Listen to me,' he said. He put his hand on Soraya's; she shrunk slightly from his touch. 'You have to tell your parents. You just have to. Ask them to forgive you. You're their flesh and blood, they have a right to know.'

'Maybe,' said Soraya quietly, so quietly Victor could hardly hear her, 'maybe if I could get up there, could actually see them, maybe it would be okay. Maybe I could stay with them until the baby's born. Till I give it up. And then make a fresh start.' She fixed her eyes on Victor's. 'Do you think that's what I should do?'

Her question hung in the air like a bubble. Victor sat very still, as if too sudden a movement might burst it.

'Yes,' he said slowly. 'I think that's exactly what you should do.'

Outside it was finally raining, and pedestrians were hurrying head down for shelter, some with umbrellas, others clutching newspapers and supermarket bags to their heads. Soraya studied a slop of coffee on the table, swooshing it in circles with her finger till it dispersed.

'There's only one problem,' she said.

She didn't actually ask Victor for the money. At least, when he thought about it afterwards, he didn't think she had. He asked how much it was she would need and she wasn't sure – two, maybe three hundred dollars for the flight. He didn't carry that kind of money. But there was the card for their Building Society account, his and Maureen's, and there was a cash machine across the road. Soraya thanked him when he returned.

'I'll never forget this,' she said. 'I don't know what I

would have done if I hadn't met you.'

But Victor couldn't help noticing her eyes sliding to his wallet, as if she were a compass, and it were her north.

Victor's bus had been inching along its route for the last five minutes, and had now stopped completely. Half a block ahead, a trolley bus was marooned, its poles broken loose from the wires. The driver was standing in the rain with a long-handled hook, trying to reattach them. He caught them, but they lurched away again.

When Victor handed Soraya the money, something had changed. He wasn't sure what. She had seemed – brisk – polite and brisk, as if they had just completed a business transaction. She had counted the money, actually counted it, six new fifty dollar notes. She left quite quickly afterwards. Victor had sat with his cold tea until one of the café staff began sweeping under his table. When her broom bumped the leg of his chair he had apologised, and gathered up his things.

The bus started to move again, the windscreen wipers struggling in the downpour. Victor wiped condensation from his window and looked out. They were passing a new development of retirement bungalows, where a rugby stadium used to stand. On a clear day, from the top, you could see all the way to the South Island. Victor had asked Soraya if he could have her parents' number, so he could call, find out how she was getting on, in seven months perhaps hear news of the baby. She had written a number on a serviette. It was in his pocket.

Victor was nearing his stop, but he didn't ring the bell. It was warm inside, and the rain was still heavy. And anyway, Maureen would not be expecting him yet. He knew how she would be: her face would set into that weary expression which he wouldn't have understood to be an expression at all if he hadn't once or twice caught sight of her without it, a Maureen altogether unfamiliar, who reminded him of someone he might have once known. He couldn't begin to think what he would tell her about the money. He decided to stay in the bus to the end of the route, and wait for it to start its return journey. But when they reached the terminus the bus driver switched off the engine and told him to get out. Through the window, Victor could see vast banks of mist and rain sweeping up the valley. The terminus was next to a children's playground, with a slide in the shape of a lighthouse and swings shuddering in the wind. On the far side of the park, a bank of toi toi shook their feathery heads, and behind them, the sea was grey and furious.

'Can I wait inside?' said Victor. 'If I buy my ticket now? I'm going back the other way.'

The driver unlatched the half-door next to his seat, leaned into the aisle and stared at him.

'This bus is not in service,' he said.

Victor nodded, put up his hood, took his carryall and his placard, and climbed down the steps. The wind whipped the rain into his face as the doors concertinaed closed. Through the glass he could see the driver was reading a newspaper.

'Not kind like you,' Soraya had said. He thought of her bare arms, her crumpled dress, the blue half moons under her eyes. He held the placard against his chest. The plastic laminate was cracking and water was leaching in grey streaks across the picture. Cars splashed past, their headlamps lighting cones of fog. Victor stood quite still, head down, water dripping from the tip of his hood, and waited for the doors to open.

Notes on Contributors

A. J. Ashworth was born and brought up in Lancashire and is a former journalist who now works in publishing. She has an MA in Writing (distinction) from Sheffield Hallam University and her stories are published or forthcoming in Horizon Review, Tears in the Fence, Crannóg, The Yellow Room, Lablit and Voices.

Alex Barr's short stories have been broadcast on Radio 4 and have appeared in magazines such as Stand. He has published two poetry collections, Letting in the Carnival (Peterloo 1984) and Henry's Bridge (Starborn 2006) and won third prize in the National Poetry Competition 2000. He is currently collaborating with Peter Oram on a translation of Rilke's French poem sequence *Vergers* and a series of books for children. He has worked as a journalist, architect and lecturer, and now lives on a small holding in West Wales with his wife Rosemarie, a ceramic artist.

Michael Coleman is a 60 year old Archive Conservator from Belfast. He has three children, three grandchildren and has been besotted, and sometimes dumbfounded, by his wife Patricia for the past 42 years. He loves sailing and jumping in puddles. He writes short stories, poetry and has a completed novel for teenagers, as yet unpublished. Michael believes in loyalty and love – and the rights of individuals to challenge society's norms.

David Frankel was born in Salford, but can now be found lurking around the darker corners of Kent, where he lives and works as an artist. He has been a secret writer most of his life, and is now working on the final stages of his first novel and a collection of short stories. He won the Earlyworks short story prize in 2009.

Adnan Mahmutovic is a Bosnian Swede, "a homely exile" who teaches literature at Stockholm University in daytime, and works with people with mental disorders at night. His book Thinner than a Hair came out in 2010 as the winner the Cinnamon Press first novel competition. His short stories have appeared in Stand, The Battered Suitcase, Rose & Thorn Journal, Cantaraville, SNR, and anthologised in [Refuge]e (Konstafack), and We're Créme de la Crem (Biscuit publ.) Website: www.adnanmahmutovic.com

Emma Martin lives in Wellington, New Zealand, arguably the windiest city in the world. She has an MA in Creative Writing from the Victoria University of Wellington. In previous lives she has been a taxi driver, circus worker and film censor.

Adrian Sells is married with a young daughter and lives in London. As a global markets strategist, his only published works to date have been in the financial press. He read English at Cambridge and, after many years recovering from the experience, now writes in his spare time. He has completed numerous short stories and is currently seeking representation for his second novel, a thriller set in South London called "Thirteen Days in Winter". Away from work and writing, he loves opera (twice a judge on the Olivier Awards opera panel) and the theatre. "Thingummy Wotsit" is first published work of fiction.

Mary O'Shea's ambition to have an ordinary life sprang, more or less directly, from one summer spent working as an undercover agent at a Butlin's Holiday Camp in North Wales, and another waiting tables at a Mafia-run restaurant in Newport, R.I. Ordinary living led her to the practice of fiction. Stories have become her passion. She published some (New Irish Writing, London Magazine), won prizes for some (Hennessy Literary Award and runner-up in the William Trevor International Short Story Competition), designed and presented a course to encourage like-minded others (U.C.C. 2005-2008). She lives with her husband, in Cork.

Angela Sherlock has worked in information retrieval, as a chef's assistant and as a (not very good) coil winder. She taught English in secondary schools in London and in Devon, where she currently resides, as wife, mother and fiction writer. Leaf Writers' Magazine has published two of her short pieces. Her first novel (as yet unpublished), The Apple Castle, was longlisted for The Virginia Prize and shortlisted for the Hookline Novel Competition. Set Dance is from her second novel, Exports, a collection of interlinked short stories about the Irish Diaspora.

Teresa Stenson's short fiction has been published in various places, most notably the 2009 Bridport Prize Winners' anthology. She is 29 and lives in York, where she balances two jobs with her writing ambitions. Along with writing short stories, Teresa is in the midst of creating a longer piece of fiction. She keeps a blog about her writing at www.teresa-stenson.blogspot.com.

Nemone Thornes was born in Dewsbury, West Yorkshire, and studied Philosophy at Newnham College, Cambridge. At nineteen, she sold her first story to The

Yorkshire Post, and her humorous short stories appeared in the Post for the following eight years. Since starting to write serious short fiction in 2007, Nemone has won prizes or been shortlisted in over twenty literary competitions. Her stories have been published by Leaf Books and Writers' Forum, and are awaiting publication at Dark Tales magazine.

Y. J. Zhu is a native of Beijing, China who now lives in San Francisco. Her first published work describes racing a motorbike across the Taklimaken Desert. She has also delivered a yacht to Mexico, sailed up the Mekong River, and cruised down the Irrawaddy River. Materials for stories come from a variety of life experience, including biking across France, exploring Angkor and Machu Picchu. She currently makes her living managing projects for financial institutions.